AF008302

ENTROPY

by
Gary Gentile

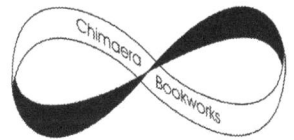

Copyright 2006 by Gary Gentile

All rights reserved. Except for the use of brief quotations embodied in critical articles and reviews, this book may not be reproduced in part or in whole, in any manner (including mechanical, electronic, photographic, and photocopy means), transmitted in any form, or recorded by any data storage and/or retrieval device, without express written permission from the author. Address all queries to:

Chimaera Bookworks
P.O. Box 57137
Philadelphia, PA 19111

Additional copies of this book may be purchased from the same address by sending a check or money order in the amount of $15 U.S. for each copy (plus $3 postage per order, not per book, in the U.S. Inquire for shipping cost to foreign countries). Alternatively, copies may be purchased from the author's website, and paid by credit card:

http://www.ggentile.com

The front cover photograph was taken by the author.

International Standard Book Numbers (ISBN)
1-883056-23-3
978-1-883056-23-0

Original copyright - 1991

Printed in the U.S.A.

Chapter 1

Sheena slipped the sword from its silvery sheath.

Danger crowded her senses. She knew that they were out there, some waiting fearfully, others closing in diffidently.

The gray forest lay shrouded in mist: a thick, clinging, moisture-laden fog that supported hordes of diminutive creatures that flitted haphazardly on gossamer wings. Dense foliage glistened with permanent dew. The ground was soft and loamy; it oozed bubbles of percolating vapor. Trees reached for the murky sky like towering monoliths whose upper branches scraped the foundations of heaven.

The sword exuded a life of its own. The burnished blade swept slowly from side to side as a warning to the encroaching skulkers.

"Sheena! Give yourself up! You are surrounded."

"And suffer the fate of dissolution?"

"We mean you no harm."

"Then leave me to my will."

"You must come back with us. Do not make our task more difficult than it already is."

"It is you who create your own troubles. Go your way, and I will go mine."

Allocution did not halt the enemy's approach. Palace guards, decidedly out of place in their filigreed finery, scuttled among the bushes. Their unfamiliarity with the terrain was obvious from the way they fumbled through shrubbery that consisted of wiry snares, snagging more than one gleaming sword or upheld pike.

"We will see that you are well cared for."

"As was my father?"

There was no reply.

Sheena carved the air with her sword as she backed across the marsh. The fog parted with each slash, leaving behind turbulent coils of condensate. She was prepared for action. Although guards slunk in each quadrant, Sheena was a long way from being entrapped.

"Let us communicate with our intellects, not our weapons." The provost parted the drooping vines and entered the clearing that Sheena defended. His regal robes were parted enough to show his armor. His sword was undrawn.

Sheena noted the tactical error. Or was it a shrewd maneuver that was intended to throw her off guard? "Against you, my sword is my envoy."

"You need not fear me."

"I do not." There was plenty of room to fight; that was the way she wanted it. "I pity you and your minions who are about to die."

"There is no pain in death, only in the fear of death. My mind suffers no anguish, my soul no fear."

"Then you will not feel this."

A sudden hinge and a quick roundhouse sweep brought the sharp edge of Sheena's sword against the provost's left torso. His ceremonial garb was severed by the blow, his armor plates cracked. Not only was he stunned, he was astonished. He did not even grab for his sword as he fell. Sheena was upon him before he hit the ground. She slipped the point of her sword under the overlapping scales of his armor.

"You cannot seriously consider murder."

"It is you who commit suicide by presumption."

"Do you intend to kill us all?"

"Only those who get in my way. The Council by its stance has decreed death for the rest. I must be free to pursue my chosen path — not for the salvation of my soul, but for the continued existence of my mind and body."

"Do you actually believe that you can change the course of the world?"

"I have no beliefs, no preconceived notions. I accept reality in whatever form it appears. The Council bandies falsehoods and misconceptions so it can retain its power. But a world in upheaval needs truth to survive."

The provost moved slightly. Sheena pressed harder.

He became very still. "I bear you no personal malice. I merely obey the Council's orders."

"But I have malice to bear, Boram. And I must leave a message that cannot be misunderstood." Sheena had the provost's full attention. "I wield but one sword, while the Council commands a guardhouse full. One less now is one less to deal with later."

The provost struggled again, but Sheena held him down with the pressure of her sword. "Please . . . "

"The time for diplomacy is past. At least your death will be quick and compassionate." She leaned against the hilt. The blade sliced easily through the unprotected flesh. The provost squirmed for the briefest moment, then stiffened, and died. "If there truly is a universal life-force, may it have mercy upon our souls."

Sheena whipped the sword from its organic sheath. There was no time to wipe off the sticky blood, for the rest of the guard squad was closing in on her. She dashed across the clearing and plunged into the forest. A surprised guard held his pike vertically in front of him, as if to ward off evil spirits. A single sideswipe from Sheena's sword cut the shaft in two. On the return sweep she slapped the flat of her sword against the guard's armor plates with enough force to bowl him over. He collapsed in a heap.

"Mercy."

The mist and miasma among the trees masked the path of her retreat. Sheena raced through the hole that she had cut in the circle of guards. It made no sense to kill innocent pawns unnecessarily. They would come after her, of that she was certain. But continuous guard work had made them soft. They were not in condition for a trek such as Sheena anticipated. Furthermore, controlling a cowardly populace did not sharpen fighting skills that had never been properly attained. Her regimen of exercise and training with the sword would stand her in good stead. She could best any palace guard in personal combat.

"Halt!"

Sheena ignored the forceful command.

The guard was slow to react.

In a flash, Sheena was beyond the protective perimeter. Little did the slow-witted guards suspect that she had allowed them to encircle her in order to demonstrate the futility of further conflict. She had escaped them once before, she could do it again just as easily.

Wraithlike she slipped through the forest. With her sword out of the way in its back-scabbard, the leafy foliage and damp brush presented no impediment. Lower tree limbs parted readily. Flying fauna danced in aerial ballet. The swamp yielded to gentle upland that was more sparsely timbered and slightly less saturated, but still the fog clung like a pall. Atmospheric humidity was constantly high — the air was practically in solution. But without the thick woodland canopy, the cloudy sky brightened to diffuse off-white. Across open sward Sheena moved rapidly, sinuously.

She soon outdistanced the guards — at least, she suspected, those who wanted to be outdistanced. A few were still on her trail: hanging back and probably waiting to determine her direction and report accordingly; they were not eager to cross swords with her, or to follow her into the wilds.

She plied a zigzag course that was intended to confuse her trackers and to lead them into trouble. From experience gained on her previous treks, Sheena knew the pitfalls of the wilderness. The world beyond the moat and castle walls was a dangerous one. Savage animals protected their domains with vicious attacks, while the untamed forests teemed with feral denizens that spouted fire and killed without abandon.

For more generations than anyone remembered, no one had ventured beyond the palisades of Erbridge into the neighboring environs. To do so invited death: if not by confrontation with the evil demons of the woods, then by Council canon. Peasants had a place in the hierarchy of the world, and that place was under direct Council dominion.

By extrapolation, Sheena was an outlaw.

Entropy

She scoffed at such a rebuke. She was not simply outside the law, she was beyond its pale. Council force existed only by dint of a few wimpish guards who, away from the confines of the castle, were hopelessly out of their element. Seldom were their orders disobeyed. Never had they been forced to chase their quarry into the wild, where Council prerogative was meaningless.

Sheena's father had challenged Council authority, and had paid the ultimate price.

Disturbed thoughts dimmed her concentration. She stopped to rest on top of a haze-covered hill. Her physical condition was superb, but the strain of flight had been difficult. She kept her senses on the alert, scanning the misty forest for the presence of her adversaries. She was prepared to fight or flee as the situation demanded: guards she could contend with, demons she was not so certain about.

It was not long before Sheena became aware of someone — or something — creeping up the slope, stalking her. She could not quite make out the shape, but she knew that demons did not creep. It was either an audacious palace guard or an ignorant savage.

Sheena unsheathed her sword. "Come forward if you do not value your life-force."

The guard tossed aside all pretense at subterfuge. Openly, purposefully, he traversed the rounded stumps that protruded randomly through the soil. He stopped out of sword range and planted the butt of his pike in the spongy grass. "I am Marek."

"Wrong. You are dead."

Marek seemed nonplussed. He loosened his grip on the pike.

"You will die the coward's way?"

He was huge, half again Sheena's size, and heavily armored, but his bulk was no match against Sheen's litheness. His cloak branded him an apprentice who grew only recently out of puberty. It was almost a shame to slay one so young.

"I offer you life, not death."

Sheena suspected a trap. He was alone, but how

many others waited in the marsh below. "I choose the latter." She brandished her sword, and approached him in a manner in which her own armor offered the most protection.

Marek spun the pike like a baton. With a speed belied by his appearance, he jammed the finely-honed tip into the ground between them. "I yield."

Sheena suspected another trick. "I can cut you down before you unsheathe your blade."

With impunity, he whipped out his dagger and flung it into the ground. The point transfixed a flat branch that lay directly in front of Sheena. "I am weaponless."

"You are mad."

"No doubt. I also have trust in your nobility."

"Trust is an unworthy possession. It is proof of either your innocence, or your ignorance."

His attitude was not one of submission. "Innocence is the pleasure of youth, ignorance the overlord's shackle."

Slowly, Sheena lowered her blade. "Where did you hear that, young guard?"

"From Wilam, your father. He was my mentor during your long absence, when it was my job to care for the needs of the Council members. He instructed me in many disciplines."

"Indeed." Sheena kept her sword in the low guard position; it was not as threatening, but just as effective. "And did he teach you trust?"

"No. He was too wise for that. He taught me never to trust."

"Then why do you repudiate his guidance?"

"Because trust in you is all I have."

Sheena admired this youth more than she liked to admit. "A curious statement coming from one who was sent to kill me. If this is a ruse — "

The ground began to vibrate. The damp soil rippled like waves on a pond, causing tufts of grass to rise and fall. Boulders were loosened from the dirt in which they were imbedded. A nearby tree shook so hard that its leaves were jostled off their stems. The entire hill undulated as if it were fluid. Marek's pike was knocked down into the low shrubbery.

"A quake!"

Sheena hardly needed confirmation of the obvious.

When the awful shaking reached its pinnacle, the ground heaved so hard that branches were shorn off the trees. Sheena and Marek reeled for stability. The tremor soon subsided. The soil lay in disjointed clumps, bushes settled down at odd angles, roots were exposed to the air. Only the fog was undisturbed.

Marek gathered himself together. "Sheena, the world is in great jeopardy. It is coming apart at the seams — caught in the grip of some mighty cosmic force."

"How do you know that?"

"Wilam confided in me before — before he passed on. He had theories — theories that were beyond my comprehension. I did not have the knowledge . . . "

"No one could, under Council dictates."

"Wilam was the Council's greatest scientist. He understood more about the world than ruling it. He was kind to me, kinder than anyone has ever been. We made a pact: he would teach if I would learn. But learning was difficult because so much of what he taught contradicted what I already knew."

"What the Council wanted you to know."

"Yes. I realize that now."

"Is that why you deserted? Is that why you sought me out?"

"I want to — offer you — my services."

Sheena pondered. "You seem a bit afraid."

"I am."

"Of me?"

"No. Of what will happen if the Council has its way."

"Good. Fear is good. It is necessary for survival."

"I am also afraid of what we will find."

"In that we agree." Sheena felt a growing compassion for the disconcerted guard. "Marek, pick up your pike and dagger."

"Then, you will let me accompany you?"

"Do you know where I go?"

"Toward hope, toward life, toward salvation. Far away from here, at the end of the world, you seek the Sacred Portal."

"Father chose you well." Sheena slid her sword back into its scabbard. "We must hurry. Time is closing in on us, and we have far to go — through the untamed forest, over the magic mountains, across the sparkling sea, and past the guarded gate. Then, not only must we find the Sacred Portal, we must unravel its secrets — before the world opens up and swallows us all."

Marek hesitated. "Sheena, how can you be certain that the Sacred Portal exists? I thought that it was a myth, like the demons that spit fire — stories to frighten children."

"Now you need more than trust. You need faith."

Chapter 2
Flashback

The tunnel appeared to go on forever.

The sparkling, crystalline walls eventually came to a point: an illusion created by distance. In fact, little Sheena had come so far that the walls converged behind her, as if the passageway were closing in and threatening to seal her off from the outside world. Still she went on, pressed by the desire to know what lay ahead, eager to learn what secrets might be divulged at the tunnel's end.

Gradually the pinpoint in front resolved itself into a finite, nebulous shape. The faceted walls were cracked, and heaps of shattered crystals littered the uneven floor. A foul, brown liquid seeped down the sides and collected in rancid puddles. Great pits in the ceiling fed growing piles of rubble that lay strewn about the disjointed pavement. Small, furred animals darted into the serenity of their nests: tiny recesses in the walls and floor.

Sheena worked her way through the breakdown until all further passage was blocked by a solid wall of ropy plastic covered with wet, slimy mud. The ceiling had collapsed, but there was no way out above because the mound of debris choked the opening. The tunnel was completely clogged.

Reluctantly, and sorely disappointed, Sheena turned back. To come so far only to be halted by an impenetrable barrier did not suit her temperament. When she began a project, she finished it; when she sought a goal, she attained it; when she asked a question, she expected a forthright answer. Frustration merely inspired her to strengthen her resolve.

She made use of the return journey by inspecting the indents in the tunnel walls. Most were shallow depressions that contained power panels, switchgear, and long-dead annunciator boards. The larger alcoves housed rusted machinery whose functions were indecipherable. At one time, she knew, the floor of the tunnel had had the ability to move; but that was in the distant past. Very little remained of the knowledge and technology used to build the castle. The ancient civilization responsible for its construction existed only in dim memory.

There was not much that Sheena could discover about the strange devices and neglected instrumentation without first understanding their overall purpose. The Ancients, as Father always allowed, did everything with a purpose — a purpose which, unfortunately, was no longer known or even suspected. Furthermore, the present Council did not desire that archaic intentions be ascertained lest they affect the status quo.

From a maintenance trough under the floor, Sheena studied the rollers that once drove the conveyor. The cylindrical steel bearings were locked in place by ages of disuse. In many places the underpinnings sagged, perhaps the result of a recent quake. Rust ran rampant.

There was technical knowledge to be gained here, but that was her father's department. Sheena was more interested in exploration, in learning the limitations of her world — and of the world outside her world. Meaning and interpretation could come later in life.

She had almost reached the outer barricade of the restricted area when a border patrol passed by. Sheena scuttled into a wall niche; she was small enough to hide in the tiniest places. The sentries made their perfunctory rounds and retreated along an intersecting tube without detecting the snickering youngster. Sheena often played hide-and-seek with the guards — always without their least suspicion. She had never been found in hiding, had never been caught sneaking after them. She was too clever.

She broached the barricade through a disguised gateway of her own making and chased after the guards. Stealthily she dashed from beam to cubbyhole, delighting in the sport of outwitting the Council's sen-

Entropy

tinels. They were oblivious to everything but their tiresome routine. Whenever Sheena approached to within throwing distance, she acted out a scenario in which she launched a pike into a guard's slovenly body. Too many times she had witnessed their brutality against defenseless people.

When Sheena grew tired of the game, she slipped up a dank, deserted trash chute that was unused and largely forgotten. She knew the hidden castle passageways better than the guards. She could hide out for ages without being discovered, or could lead a chase indefinitely. The chute led her to an empty storage compartment. She slipped behind a loose grille into a ventilator shaft interconnected with a complex of vertical chimneys. Ascending the proper flue eventually brought her up to street level near the castle's outer wall.

A solo sentinel, practically obscured in the mist, lounged in the lofty tower, while a few perimeter guards meandered along the empty ramparts. The drawbridge had not been lowered in anyone's memory, and it was doubtful that its motors still operated.

Undetected, she charged into the knotted foliage of the park, delighting in the cover it offered. With reckless abandon, she raced through the woods, ducked under low-slung limbs, vaulted over narrow streams, and took care to avoid dense undergrowth that might slow her progress. Narrow paths wound through the garden, but presented no challenge to the explorer in training.

The first intersecting roadway was deserted. Sheena slipped across the broad swath like an escaped prisoner, knowing full well that if caught, she would merely be scolded for playing out of bounds. She felt a resurgence of freedom as she entered the next tract of woodland, but it did not last for long. The forest thinned to scattered groves and sparse, unkempt grass. Pavements and glidebelts took the place of hard-packed clay.

She wandered along the byways, some of which still groaned along on worn rollers, and worked her way toward the grand Citadel whose upper stories were wreathed in mist. Maintenance crews, messengers, and workers on prescribed errands flooded the streets. Sheena melded with the crowd like other youngsters with no appointed rounds. When she reached the Citadel's ornate rampart, she paused in reflection: she had gone farther underground than the distance over land to the outer walls. *She had been outside the castle.* Sheena was ecstatic. Her mother would be proud of her.

She passed through a privileged gate into the Citadel's magnificent courtyard. Her familial badge was recognized so the sentries paid her no mind. She scampered by haughtily, knowing full well that she could have sneaked past them had she chosen. She zigzagged around ornate obelisks as if they were part of an obstacle course, pausing momentarily at the fountain where she so often played with her toy boats ingeniously propelled by a bellows pumping air onto hanging cloths.

The entrance dome was so spacious that parts of it were obscured by mist that filtered in through the latticework vents. Great metallic pendants hung on thick cables from the gilded ceiling. Gold and silver ornaments decorated the curved marble walls. The marblelike floor was inlaid with polished strips of wood. The honor guard, still as statues, wore uniforms that sparkled with jewels and precious stones. A broad, balustraded ramp spiraled around the inside of the spherical structure. Crystals fed by the moisture-laden atmosphere grew on the exposed surfaces.

As a Council member, Wilam occupied one of the uppermost floors of the Citadel. In many ways, life was easier at the top: less physically demanding with more privileges than accorded to lowlanders and cavedwellers. Wilam had his own private chamber, and shared retinue with the other Council members. Sheena found him engrossed in study at his computer terminal. She sneaked up behind him and gave him a firm embrace.

Wilam disconnected himself from the input-output

electrodes. "How is my baby?"

"I am not a baby."

"All right, then. What are you?"

"I am —I am —a juvenile. No! An adolescent."

"Ha-ha-ha. You think highly of yourself, as most precocious striplings do. But you will always be *my* baby no matter what age either of us attains."

"That is not fair!"

"Perhaps not. But in this world, it is the least unfair treatment you are likely to receive. Remember that when you grow up."

"I told you — "

"I know. In your own mind you are already grown up, nearly ready to be apprenticed."

"I do not want to be apprenticed. I want to help carry on your work."

Wilam ruffled his robe. "Ah, you desire to become a Council member."

"And why not?"

"Perhaps because the feminine gender has never been granted such a position."

"That is no reason."

"Worse than that, it is unreasonable. But that is the way it is, whether or not you and I approve."

"Then it is time for a change."

"Ah, the young lady who would move the world to suit her fancy." Wilam thought for a moment. "Yes, I daresay there are some major faults in our world. In fact, according to my calculations, serious transformations are taking place that are quite beyond our control."

"The Council already overexercises its authority."

"Ah, the naive politician whose lack of diplomacy may sometime lead to her downfall."

"Executive privilege goes too far. It takes neither an adult nor a genius to behold the inequity of the system."

"So the precocious child becomes the brash elder. To express such thoughts is heresy."

"Truth is heresy only to those who choose beliefs

over facts."

Wilam was a doting as well as a tolerant father. "Already I have disfavored the Council's graces with my opinions. I am no longer trusted even though my scientific studies declare only revelation, not revolution; even though the changes I refer to are not acts of Council, but of natural law."

Sheena was nonplussed.

"And that, my baby, is something that you are still too young to understand. Even I — "

A messenger appeared at the door.

"Pardon me a moment." Wilam left his daughter and approached the messenger, feigning anger. "How dare you enter my chambers unannounced."

"I am sorry, sire. I did not know you were engaged."

"It is not necessary for you to know my business, only to show respect."

"I apologize."

"Do not let it happen again." Wilam confronted him long enough for his intimidation to be felt. "What is so important that you discard good manners?"

"If you please, sire, a notice of meeting to discuss the diversion of personnel from nonessential duties to Citadel reconstruction crews."

"Everything is essential, not just rebuilding fortifications destroyed by natural disaster. Who do they think we are protecting ourselves from?" The question was purely rhetorical. "Very well, I will be along shortly." Wilam dismissed the irreverent messenger.

He departed hastily.

Dropping his veil of annoyance, Wilam returned to his computer console. "I dislike being rude, but I fear that rival Council members send informers in the guise of messengers. My investigations are drawing too much attention for the political infrastructure to bear."

"But what is wrong with revealing facts?"

"Sheena, if you are to survive this topsy-turvy world of ours, you must learn — and accept — that everything is not as it seems. We are moving backward: our machines break down, and our mechanics cannot repair them; our buildings collapse, and our craftsmen are unable to restore them; our communications fail, and our technicians tell us to use messengers. We have had no outside contact in ages; we do not even know if others still live in a land presumed to have regressed to a state primeval. The Council repudiates such knowledge: as long as we remain in our impregnable castle, they allege we are safe — as if insularity ensures security. They ignore the forces that can kill at a distance, the periodic upheavals that shake the very foundations of our world.

"We are losing wisdom at an accelerating pace, yet my fellow Council members scorn me for resurrecting the science of the past. We are descendants of a race that achieved great technological feats, yet we squander our heritage on preserving aristocratic supremacy. We are stifling in an intellectual vacuum, yet the Council promotes ignorance because it guarantees domination over the masses."

Sheena interrupted his diatribe. "Now who expresses heresy?"

"Quite right, my baby. Quite right." Wilam indicated the computer console. "All the knowledge of the Ancients is locked inside this electronic storehouse. The secrets of the Universe are there for the taking. Yet, while I toil to decipher the codes and search the files for data, my fellow leaders pursue a worthless life of mental amusement and physical pleasure. As the world collapses around us, they are hard at play."

"In that respect, Father, we are of the same mind."

"And in many respects you take after your mother." After a pause, he added thoughtfully, "I just wish she were still alive."

Chapter 3

Marek stabbed his pike through the leaves of a bush. "Something moved in there."

"Beyond the castle moat, the outer world houses many strange beings."

"So I begin to understand. And are these things dangerous?"

"Some of them." Sheena traveled with litheness that exaggerated Marek's lumbering movements. "But when they are, you will know it long before you get close enough to poke at them. Only imaginary threats stay still."

"Do I seem so guileless?"

"No more than anyone untrained in woodcraft and inexperienced at delivering death." Sheena indicated Marek's dagger. "Have you ever had blood on your blade?"

"Not yet."

"Would you have killed someone?" Sheena pointed in the direction of the castle. "Back there?"

"If ordered."

"Without thinking?"

"I was trained to act on command."

"Then understand that from now on, you take your orders from me, and act on *my* command. To disobey could mean death — certainly for you, possibly for both of us."

"Would you slay me for disobedience?"

"No. For lack of confidence in my judgment. Your sinecure with the Council did not prepare you for a journey into the wilderness."

"And how did you come to be so prepared?"

The swamp lay sheathed in a vaporous atmosphere that obscured the treetops, but hung only in wisps along the soggy bottom. Giant leaves drooped like green parasols. Rotting logs lay strewn across the ground, some straddling unctuous puddles like rounded bridges. In single file, with Sheena in the lead, they sloshed through the wet bottomlands.

"My mother trained me as a tot. She taught me to be strong, resilient, resourceful. The rest I learned on my own."

"What you toss off in a few curt sentences is a lifetime of discipline."

"Not quite a lifetime, unless you compare your life to mine. I am twice your age."

"And you have spent much of that time in the feral lands beyond the moat — a bane to the Council, a boon to the masses. Your name — "

"Enough!"

Shallow rivulets merged into a deep, slow-moving stream. Sheena waded across to the loamy bank opposite. Marek hesitated.

"Why do you wait?"

Marek surveyed the patches of green sludge that covered the rippling surface. There was movement in the floating islands. "What is that — stuff?"

Sheena made light of his discomfiture. "Nothing but lowly fungus. It will not hurt you." She snapped a branch off a nearby tree, stuck it into one of the viscous rafts of vegetation, and held it aloft. A string of primordial jelly drooled off the stick and was absorbed into the stream without a splash. "You will soon learn that you have little to fear from nature's kingdom. Those creatures that are harmful do not attack; they act only in self-defense. Avoidance is the best tactic."

Marek slipped into the slime, cringing. "I do not like this."

"Neither will the palace guards. That is why we come this way."

Marek's disgust was not so easily allayed. "But there are things — creeping — in this muck."

Sheena appreciated the humor of the situation. "Things that are more afraid of you than you are of them."

"Do not be so certain of that." Marek emerged from the stream obviously shaken. "I do not like creepy, crawly things."

"You will get used to them. You have no choice." Strange feelings stirred inside her: emotions she had never experienced, and therefore did not recognize. For all his size and physical strength Marek was so child-like. At this age in her solitary life, was she finally giving in to mothering instincts?

Young Marek brushed himself off. With resolve, "Yes, I suppose I must."

"There is no need to apologize for not enjoying unfamiliar conditions." Sheena might have been making excuses for herself rather than for Marek. "My first river crossing was equally unlikable."

"Ah, so you do have chinks in your armor."

Sheena rattled her breastplate. She realized the trap she had gotten herself into. Ingenuous though this lad might be, he was also astute. "Father chose you well. You even mimic his affectations."

Once free of all vestiges of slimy fungus, Marek expressed glee. "Wilam told me that I must, in order to win you over. You do not make friends easily."

"You risk offending me with your honesty."

"No, you can be offended only by dishonesty."

"You appear to know me well — perhaps too well."

"I know only what your father told me. He loved you."

"As I loved him." What was this young guard doing to her? In the short time since they had met she felt more unease than she had in her entire life. She was naked without anger and hatred. "I think learning will be a painful process for both of us. Come. We must keep on the move. I fear the castle minions may pick up our trail."

"With Boram dead, do you think the rest will follow?"

Sheena hacked a swath through the dense brush. "They are near us even now. But without his guidance they will be loathe to attack. Who is next in command?"

"Charel."

"A coward who hides behind the robes of others:

ever resourceful but never bold."

"Perhaps when you knew him last. But he has come into power since your first departure, and has overcome his diffidence. If he proves his worthiness to the Council, they will make him their leader."

They broke into a broad clearing swathed in mist, matted with grass, and dotted with tall hummocks of dirt. Sheena plucked a tuft of green blades, wiped sap off the flat of her sword, and returned the blade to its sheath. "Marek, you may prove useful to me yet. Knowledge of one's enemy — "

The hummocks erupted like miniature volcanoes. Long sinuous animals without appendages arced into the air and hit the ground flowing like loose lava. Fangs gnashed threateningly. Individual members slithered over each other, a rolling carpet fringed with daggerlike teeth.

Sheena's sword slashed. "Stay your ground!"

Marek was already halfway through the brush. He turned at her command, and led his charge with his pike. Together they hacked at the scaled creatures that assaulted them unprovoked. The frail, slender bodies separated easily. A few got past Sheena's swift sword; her dress was shredded in several places, but her armor protected her body. Marek suffered similarly. Soon the arena was littered with gore and the soil was stained with blood. The routed army that slunk back into the holes was significantly fewer in number.

"Well done." She flipped over one of the bodies to reveal its nasty armament. "They are highly territorial."

Marek exhibited undisguised dismay. "Is it always like this in the wilderness?"

"No." Sheena once again wiped grass across shiny steel. "It is usually worse. But cheer up. You performed well."

"I fear *your* wrath more than theirs."

Sheena was amused. This youth had more courage than he cared to admit. She casually sheathed her blade as she crossed the vanquished sward. "Fear me not as long as you act with valor."

He followed along behind her. "And was this a test?"

Once again Sheena found herself astonished by her companion's shrewdness. She had already paid him enough compliments, so she offered no praise. "I have skirmished with these beasts before." She knocked dirt off a hummock in passing. "They rely on shock value to drive off intruders, but are too small to harm us."

Marek dragged his pike through the grass until all vestige of blood and gore was gone. "A behavior pattern of great value. But, why do I have no knowledge of them? They do not appear on any learning programs."

"Most of what we will encounter will be new to you." They exited the glade onto a tree-lined trail roofed with large fronds bowed by the weight of rigid cusps. "The world is full of unfamiliar plants and alien creatures whose form and life cycles are beyond your imagination."

Marek ducked under the spiked leaf-tips. "How can that be? Where did they come from? How did they get here?"

The path led down to more damp swamp.

"All good questions. Your curiosity has not been dampened by Council brainwashing. Father — " Sheena paused to examine a crushed log and a queer depression that cut a narrow swath through the grassy undergrowth.

Marek stopped by her side, and explored a hedgerow with his pike. "What is it? Machines of the Council's guards?"

"Be still!"

Marek froze.

A preternatural calm suffused the marshland. The air did not move, the trees did not creak. Gone were the countless small critters that constantly flitted about.

"Follow me! Quickly!"

Sheena struck out through the clinging morass, ignoring thickets and shallow pools. Marek was right behind her. Only a moment passed before a moss-covered trunk burst into flames and showered the ground with bark and bits of blazing debris. Branches became fiery brands, leaves were turned to ash.

"For your life, hurry!"

Marek did not have Sheena's speed and mobility. She gradually outdistanced him, accelerating as she raced uphill. The high ground was firm and sparsely packed with low vegetation. A grove of saplings exploded violently, spewing sawdust and scorched soil into a broiling, incandescent cloud.

"A demon!" Marek had a knack for noting the obvious.

The amorphous mass that came after them was monstrous: thrice the height of Marek and double his girth. Grotesque features were intermittently occluded by a mask of self-generated steam. Heat waves shimmered around a scaled, bulbous body. The demon crushed and singed everything in its path as it rumbled through the thick copse. A blast of flame belched from its midriff and instantly incinerated a clump of shrubbery.

Sheena reached the base of a tall bluff where naked rock bulged in jagged relief above the undergrowth. Sharp, slender pinnacles rose high enough to stab the clouds. Stunted trees crowded the entrance to a broad overhang.

"Into that cave."

The demon snorted flame from an upper orifice that was shrouded in smoke. Long appendages flailing from the rounded trunk grappled with low-hanging branches, snapping thick limbs as if they were sticks. Burning trees were bowled over like blades of grass.

Sheena fought through a wall of thick, hanging vines just as another ball of fire gouged the cliff front. Melted crystal and beads of molten rock burst outward. Marek dodged the worst of it, caught the fringes with his armor. He stamped out smoldering portions of his uniform as he crashed through the woody barrier into the shallow shelter. Sheena disappeared into a constriction in the back of the recess. Quickly she spun an override wheel, forced open a hatch on squeaky hinges, and entered a small chamber. Crystals glittered on rough-hewn rock. "Get in here."

Marek obeyed. "Where does it lead?"

"Away from *that*."

With the dreaded unknown ahead but certain death behind, Marek helped close the vault's hatch. "You have my faith."

Sheena deftly spun the locking wheel. "We are safe. It will not come in here."

Marek was tremulous. "How can you be certain?"

"They are programmed not to."

Chapter 4
Flashback

"I am too old for this, Sheena."

"Nonsense, Father. You are wasting away at your console. These excursions into the basements are good for you. The exercise will keep you trim and help you gain some much-needed weight."

"All this does is tire me. The lower planes are no place for a sickly man, for any material gains are quickly lost. I do better to concentrate on mental exercises. The activity of the brain increases when the body begins to fail. Besides, you are every bit as qualified as I to calibrate the equipment."

"As qualified, yes; but not as experienced. Besides, in order to maintain the route for my return, you must know my means of exfiltration. I do not fancy crossing the moat and climbing the outer bulwark. Unobservant as they are, the guards cannot fail to miss so obvious an approach."

Wilam ticked off his arguments in defense. "Your prowess is uncanny, your skill with the sword unexcelled. A guard in your way will be dispatched in a trice. I expect to train a young protégé to manage the actual maintenance. I have followed your map faultlessly to this very airlock. And experience is not necessary with so simple a device."

Sheena could not hide her mirth. "Your oratory is as cutting as my sword. You can kill with debate. Yet, despite your admonitions, you came with me. Why?"

Wilam placed the gravitometer on the floor beside the hatch. He fiddled with the dials and adjusted the settings. He became very serious. "A long time ago I saw your mother off on the same adventure. She departed openly, but in a cloud of suspicion and mixed emotion because of her avowed purpose. I continued my vigilance, especially as her homecoming would not be met with accord. The Council has stated its position in that regard."

Recollections of her mother were faint in Sheena's mind. She *felt* more than she remembered. Katha was a woman full of life, desire, and ambition. She often displayed emotion, but was dominated by an inner resolve manifested by sheer will and the precepts of logic. She was resourceful, and knew how to get what she wanted. She lived every moment with intensity.

"You must have loved her very much, Father. Why did you let her go on such a dangerous journey?"

"For the same reason I am letting you go — because I have no choice in the matter. You will do what you want."

"You have always encouraged such conduct."

"My baby, you confuse encouragement with lack of dissuasion. There is a great deal of your mother in you, and with that heritage goes a larger purpose in life than mere existence. You have your own destiny to find. Far be it for me to get in your way."

"That unselfishness demonstrates more love than — "

Wilam interrupted her. "You exalt me falsely. My motives are baser than you would like to believe. In a world that is flying apart at the seams there are more important things than love. Carry this thought with you on your travels: perhaps your fascination for adventure was influenced by my own aspirations. You are not just my baby, but an extension of myself and my goals."

"If that is true, it is because the survival of the world is more important to you than personal comfort."

"You will not let me be less than perfect, will you?"

"You must be what you are."

"And you are what I cannot be. While I delve into the data banks and explore the safe depths of imagination, you will be engaging real physical danger. That was your mother's spirit; that is your greatest faculty. My greatest weakness is that I am afraid. I dread these deep planes. I am terrified at the thought of placing myself in a position of peril. Even though my body shrivels and weakens, the contemplation of eternal rest hurts more than the pain of life."

"Yet you fight the Council without qualm."

"But I know the odds, and can calculate the outcome. You are going out into the great unknown."

"With eager anticipation." Sheena cranked open the reluctant hatch. "Enough maudlin philosophizing. You must return before you are missed, I must be far away before a search party can be organized if the scrofulous guards dare to come after me."

Wilam pulled his daughter close and hugged her tight. "I love you Sheena, my not-so-little baby." He refused to let her go. "I want to spend every possible moment with you, in case I leave this plane of existence before your return. I feel so weak."

Sheena forced him away. "Nonsense, Father. A little rest will restore your strength." She indicated the recording instrument. "Do not forget your measurements."

"I have done so already." He pulled a radiation counter from his pack and placed the apparatus on the dirt-covered deck. "Never before have I been so far underground. I must take advantage of the moment."

"I will do the same." Sheena slipped through the opening and slowly swung the hatch. "Good bye, Father. I love you."

"I love you, Sheena. And remember, only a quick exploratory — " She closed and locked the hatch.

The long abandoned maintenance tunnel continued on the other side of the airlock through crystal-studded sandstone. Power cables and uninsulated bus bars crowded both walls. Through the copper conductors flowed high-voltage electricity that could arc, and incinerate the unwary at a distance. Sheena kept to the middle of the corridor despite the transparent barriers that prevented unauthorized access to the energized transmission lines.

Soon she reached an intersection where eight tubes met like the spokes of a wheel. Massive switchgear filled the cathedral-like hub. Sheena quickly traversed the room to the tunnel she had previously marked, and followed it to a vertical shaft encircled by a ramp. She ascended to a higher plane, wound through a maze of hallways and storage closets, and located the ramp that led upward to a double-door airlock. She emerged from the external hatch far beyond the castle walls.

The ever-present fog clung like a pall.

The soil was moist yet firm, and supported exotic varieties of plant life unknown within the confines of the castle. More interesting was the proliferation of bizarre fauna that inhabited the forest. Nothing in Wilam's teachings had prepared her for that. Nothing in the data banks had warned of their existence.

The pudgy bundle of flesh Sheena first encountered appeared as curious about her as she was about it. The bowl-sized body was covered with horny plates, much like her own armor, and scampered along the grass on eight flabby appendages that writhed in sequence. A similar but larger version climbed trees on tentacles surrounded by pointed knots. Another launched itself from the upper canopy, and floated gently to the ground on spread appendages attached by flaps of soft, flexible scales.

Colonies of dwarfish animals occupied the knolls that rose high into the cloud layer. They guarded holes that Sheena suspected led to underground burrows. When she shooed them with the flat of her sword, they scuttled into their subterranean homes. Sheena soon learned that almost any animal could be chased away simply by beating the bush.

The strange world outside the castle was different from anything Sheena could have imagined. More than an extension of the encircling forest, the terrain undulated randomly through dense brush, soggy marsh, and open prairie.

At first Sheena wandered almost aimlessly: she was happy to be free from the bonds of confinement, from the restrictions of the Council. She scrutinized each bush, studied each plant, climbed the bark-studded trees, probed the damp morass, and stole after the outlandish creatures that inhabited this peculiar region of

Entropy

the world.

Gradually she refined her rambling to a direction. As straight as possible in a land filled with obstacles, she struck out unimpeded on a course her father had selected after careful examination of the records. The coriolimeter pointed the way. She did not know what she might find out there — did not want to know until she arrived. This was a game to her — like exploring the tunnels as a little girl, and avoiding the dull-witted guards.

A lance of fire flashed through the air and drilled through the base of a tree. Sheena was showered with bark and beads of hot sap. The thing that emerged from the brush did not resemble any kind of animal Sheena had ever met. It was half her size, and skittered on rigid tentacles jutting from the flanks of a plated, angular body.

In a burst of speed, Sheena ducked for cover and drew her sword. Another bolt of fire singed the grass at the spot she had just vacated. The thing was many sword-lengths away. Against a weapon that worked at a distance, Sheena was forced to retreat. She vacated the thicket an instant before it was transfixed with a radiant beam of pure energy that sent galvanic shivers through her body. She dashed through a hedgerow and across a clearing to a grove of trees whose trunks were connected with horizontal ligaments.

The monster would not let her escape. It came after her, spitting packets of electricity that blackened the ground and boiled away puddles. A threadlike condensation trail momentarily pierced the air after every blast. Sheena knew exactly where the thing was, but not how to kill it. The only choice left was to outwit it.

Chased by bolts that sizzled through the air uncomfortably close, she sought either refuge or a way of disabling her unnatural opponent. Not until she came across a rock outcrop did she find an escape route. The airlock frame had been disjointed by a not-too-recent tremor. The hatch lay on the ground partially buried under dirt and growing grass.

She cowered in the inner chamber as the energy-wielding monster drew near. The quake that had destroyed the outer hatch had also twisted the inner frame out of shape, jamming the hatch. With further retreat blocked, Sheena held her sword outthrust and waited to do battle. She flattened herself against the rock wall next to the outer opening, and prepared to deliver a quick downward slash through her attacker's electric sword.

The monster spit and sputtered beyond the opening, and skewed back and forth as if looking for an advantage; but it did not come close. The blue-white coruscation on the tip of its nozzle-like blade grew dimmer by the moment. The thing rocked gently on two paddlewheel-type appendages that could have passed for spoked wheels without rims. Sheena had the impression that it might be thinking.

Whatever conceptual process was occurring within the lumpish body, the thing carried away with it. It trundled off through the forest occasionally lashing out mildly with its electric beam.

Sheena gradually pulled herself together. For the first time in her life she experienced an emotion her mother had told her about: fear. She trembled in the release of pent-up terror, for a long time immobilized by the after-effects of her near demise. When she finally regained control of her functions, she experienced only a brief moment of relief before her feelings swung into full-blown anger.

Worse than the feeling of fear was the realization that she had given in to it.

Sheena charged out of the airlock bent on revenge against the creature that had forced her into the predicament of self-actualization. She easily caught up to it, for its gait had slowed considerably and its course became more aberrant. Sheena stalked it with savage intent. Finally, what first appeared to be a meandering, pointless route, resolved into a pattern. The thing seemed to be methodically searching the forest.

It stopped in the middle of a small clearing packed

Entropy

with dense, spongy moss and surrounded by tall trees hung with broad, flat fronds. With its two sets of rigid tentacles spinning in opposite directions, the thing whirled in a circle and created a draft that washed away a patch of moss. When it ceased moving, a flexible appendage snaked out of its abdomen, felt along the ground, and plugged itself into a recessed socket. The faint coruscation faded from its nozzle. The ground vibrated.

Sheena had never killed but she had often dreamt of it. She took advantage of the moment of stillness. Leading her onslaught by the tip of her sword, she dashed across the clearing at her fastest speed and plunged the blade into the offensive monster. The sword ricocheted like steel on steel, cutting a shallow divot along the thing's outer shell but otherwise not penetrating the body.

Sheena had not anticipated such an event. Her momentum had carried her past the thing and in front of the death-dealing nozzle. For the briefest moment she hesitated between immediate withdrawal and uncertain attack. Then she whipped her blade in a sweeping arc that brought the length of it hard against the thing's tough hide.

The monster remained upright but was knocked aside, its tentacles gouging tracks in the moss. Sheena's tempered blade bit deeply into the thing's body. But when she pulled back her sword no blood flowed; a deep dent marked the thing's hidden armor. The nozzle began to arc.

She slashed again, this time at the tip of the thing's fantastic weapon; it sheered off completely. Knowing at least that the monster was not invulnerable, she swung at its spokelike tentacles. The blade chopped through the rigid extensions only after repeated swipes. When at last she sliced through the lower tentacles, the thing fell over, wrenching the flexible lower appendage out of the ground. A flash of electricity burst from the socket, leaped the gap of the severed connection, and exploded against the thing's lower abdomen.

The monster was ripped apart. Scraps of hide, pieces of tentacle, and chunks of oily viscera were splattered indiscriminately across the clearing. Sheena flattened herself to the ground. Her armor protected her from most of the flying debris, but she suffered numerous small cuts and a few deep wounds. When she picked herself up, she surveyed the fractionated remains of the monster.

The thing was not organic.

The parts scattered in the moss or imbedded in bark were either metal or plastic. In place of organs it had servomotors; for a brain it had a microprocessor; the steel chassis housed belts for direct current generation, and capacitors for electrical storage.

If Wilam's computer failed to describe the variety of wildlife beyond the castle walls, most of it harmless, it never even hinted at hostile mechanical entities.

Sheena gathered all the recognizable pieces. Wilam would be ecstatic.

Chapter 5

"A machine?" Marek was incredulous. "You mean the demon was a machine?"

"Technically, a robot. Battery operated and remotely controlled."

"The demons are controlled? But how?"

"In a fashion unknown. Because it was a small unit with limited reserves, it soon depleted its stored power. I caught it at a charging port defenseless and unaware. The larger units are not so easily defeated or de-energized."

Marek practically filled the chamber with his bulk. His pike cut the corners diagonally. "Are all the demons just — mechanical devices?"

"Without disdain, yes, but very sophisticated."

"And they are not — supernatural?"

"On the contrary. But neither are they natural. They are constructs."

"Made by whom?"

"That is what we hope to find out." Sheena squeezed past the naive apprentice. On the opposite side of the room was a hatch identical to the one through which they had entered. She led Marek through it onto a platform whose rounded lip became a steep ramp that angled down through the mountainside. The tunnel was as high and as wide as her body; Marek was forced to scrunch himself together in order to penetrate the conduit. Glittering grains of sand studded the interior of the tube.

"How did you know about this place?"

"I did not. I know of others like it, and I recognized the entrance."

"What is it?" Marek wanted to know.

"An access shaft."

"Is it artificial?"

"Built by the Ancients." Sheena paused intermittently to inspect indentations in the walls.

Marek noticed the plastic insets that crowded the notches. "Proximity switches."

"Yes, but long inactivated. There is no one to warn at the end of the shaft."

"And where does it go?"

"To one of the deep planes."

Far beneath the surface, the ramp broadened and leveled, then entered a cavern scintillating with crystalline formations. Massive square columns joined floor to roof in a purely functional manner. Piles of rubble stood high under irregular ceiling fractures; fissures in the pavement yawned like craters. A defunct annunciator panel dangled at the end of a bundle of sheathed cables, and was surrounded by broken gauges and crumbling machinery.

Marek was agog. "It is like the tunnels beneath the castle, only many times larger."

"It is not just a tunnel, but a subsurface highway system."

"Out here? In the wilderness?"

"In the remote past, all the castles were interconnected with underground thoroughfares."

"There are other castles? But I thought . . . "

After a pause, Sheena finished for him, "You thought ours was the only castle in the world. You probably also think the woods are inhabited by savages."

"Of course. Who else but savages groveling in caves could survive against the demons?" He added hastily, "Even if they are machines."

"Anyone with intelligence, a little perception, and some knowledge of their workings. Not everyone in the world is as ignorant as the Council has kept the lower classes. Most of the so-called savages — the people who live outside the castle — are masters of their environment."

"I thought only the Ancients possessed power over the forces of nature. How can mere savages possess such influence?"

"I can enlighten you, Marek, if you are willing to

Entropy

break the bonds of false doctrine bestowed upon you by the Council."

"In that I am willing."

"Denouncing preconceived notions is a painful process."

"Wilam has impressed that upon me already."

Sheena took a moment to reflect on her father. "He was a good man — a great man — with one of the best minds produced in many generations."

"Better than yours?"

"Possibly. But, as great as he was, he had his limitations."

"We all do."

"Most, anyway." Sheena paused at the edge of an elevated roadbed. The top lamination was constructed of corrosion-resistant metal that shone as if just forged. Plastic bearings showed the wear of extended usage; a thick sediment of dust attested to the long period of disuse.

"What is this structure?"

Sheena ascended a ramp to the level of the road. The heavy-duty metal could have supported a thousand times her weight. She preceded Marek along the unyielding surface. "A conveyor belt."

"A slidewalk wider than the Citadel's courtyard? Impossible."

"It was not made to carry people, but freight. Vessels full of supplies were transported by subway to all parts of the world. The Ancients lived on a grand scale. Once, all the castles belonged to a vast network under single cooperative rule."

"And have you visited these other castles?"

"A few. Most are abandoned, and lie in ruins; those that are occupied are in only slightly better repair — their people have forgotten more than we about our origins."

"And you escaped with your life?"

Sheena kept moving at a pace which, in these nether regions, Marek found difficult to keep. Rock falls required constant negotiation. Sheena ignored the strange devices and ungainly contrivances that lined the walls and filled the alcoves. "The so-called savages may be ignorant of their past, but they are more civilized than you imagine. What they lack in technology they make up for with quite advanced cultures and subtle art. Individual freedom is the norm."

"The Council would not permit such a state. And a system of shared control would be anathema."

"A feudal society is a futile society. Either it will be overthrown by the malcontents, or it will perish from indifference. Our castle is strongly ruled by decadent leaders, and its people are spiritless. It coasts gently toward self-destruction at a pace that is quickly accelerating. The Council refuses to recognize this fact. While the foundations collapse, they practice their sybaritic rites."

Marek shuddered. "I fear such blasphemy even though we are alone."

"You know it is true, but worse is what you do not know. We are on the brink of technological extinction. When the last machine breaks, when the final computer goes down, then the castle becomes a prison. For generations people have feared to leave it; so they will perish. On a greater scale the entire world is dying. Without technology and the knowledge of its workings, we are all doomed."

"You spin riddles."

A jagged crevasse gaped before them. Out of its unplumbed depths rose sparkling dirt and crystalline dust, carried upward by a steady draft. The airborne debris was deflected by the ceiling. Granulated snow spread outward, then fell twinkling onto the smooth surface of the road. Drifts of cold fluff lined both sides of the narrow chasm.

"I do not spin riddles, I merely relate them." Sheena thoughtfully surveyed the scene before them. "This is curious."

Marek cautiously approached the slippery edge. The breeze ruffled his robe. "What causes it?"

"I do not know. But it must be a recent phenome-

Entropy

non. Notice how the dunes build in height? Father could undoubtedly calculate the rate of growth and extrapolate backward to the beginning of the event. I venture to guess that it would coincide with a recent quake."

"You mean that vapors are being released from a crack in the world's mantle?"

Sheena stayed away from the barrier dune, but studied the eddies close to the cavern's side where air was being siphoned over the brink. "So it would appear. Yet, at the same time another current is being drawn downward — as if the air were circulating."

"Is that possible?"

"Without understanding the mechanisms responsible, I will not venture to guess. We will log it as an observation without conclusion. Come, let us continue." Sheena jumped the crevasse at one extremity, where it was the narrowest. She waited for Marek to join her. "Come."

Marek halted a moment before leaping across the angular slit from one polished surface to the other. He fell just short enough to dislodge loose rubble that fell into the seemingly bottomless abyss. He was not unruffled by the close call. "My strength is failing. I feel as if the walls and ceiling are pressing down upon me."

"The depths of these caverns affect the body as much as the mind. You must overcome your weakness."

Marek leaned against his pike. "Lead on. I will not hold you back."

Once again Sheena admired Marek's inner resolve. "The burden of these abandoned caves is preferable to the onslaught of demons. Besides, travel is so much faster." She sped off to prove her point.

Marek did his best to keep up. They detoured the largest piles of rubble, and several times climbed down from the road to the maintenance track when their route was blocked. Once, where a section of wall was missing, colorful sandstone and mineral deposits created a shallow talus. Tangled tree roots hung down into the open space where the ground had fallen away.

Later, they came upon a deserted underground station. Compartments fitted with long-dead computer terminals dominated the depot, while storage chambers and living quarters occupied the outskirts. Motors motionless for generations lay smothered under strata of accumulated rust.

Marek brandished his pike. "Did Wilam know these places?"

"Father's knowledge was limited to what he found in the data banks, and what information I brought back from my first trek — the mechanical monsters, the strange wildlife, the world's natural wonders. When I returned from my second outing . . . " Sheena meandered aimlessly, exploring with little interest.

Marek waited appropriately before breaking her reverie. "Sheena, he was onto something — at the end. Even before your second reappearance, he made some fundamental discovery which caused great dissension among the Council. And, if you believe it, some of the members shifted to his side."

Sheena stumbled on. "I had only a few moments with him before . . . "

"I know. Your presence created an uproar, and events moved quickly. But, while you were gone, Wilam was working on an — an imaginary equation, as he put it: some reversal in physics in which the world is gripped. When you arrived, he was close to discovering what he called the ultimate truth of our world. And although he did not divulge it to me, it was more terrifying to him than an entire horde of mechanical demons. For a long time he was up against a barrier in data access — a barrier he was about to broach. He put it all on crystal. Then — "

Sheena halted at a barrier no less physical than Wilam's: this one metallic, not electronic. The wall extended completely across the tunnel, from floor to ceiling; it was solid and impenetrable.

Marek leaned his bulk against the shiny surface. "There are no cracks or seams."

Entropy

"They all end this way — as if the Ancients had a ban against building roads too long and continuous."

"Must we return? To a gate guarded by an angry demon?"

"Every wall has a chink, every obstacle a bypass." Sheena paused in thought. "Except the wall at the end of the world."

"A strange admission for a heretic."

"I have been there. I have touched the wall."

"You mean — the legends are true?"

"Behind every legend lies truth greatly exaggerated. I will tell you about it . . . "

Chapter 6

Flashback

The swamp seemed endless.

How long Sheena had been crossing the wetlands was impossible to know. She had long since lost track of time.

Half-submerged logs and decaying vegetation provided an eerie backdrop for exotic creatures that drifted in ichorous pools, or soared through the clinging mist-laden air. Ripples from her passing disturbed clusters of floating fronds. Colonies of air-filled, bubble-shaped animals, each propelled by tiered rows of cilia, scattered at her approach. The bog was alive with myriad forms of life.

Although she was nearing the end of her strength, the thick, swirling miasma sustained her resolve to keep moving. She could not rest in the depths of the swamp. So she kept searching for some break in the horizontal monotony, a rise to dry ground.

Eventually gurgling streamlets drained into an unctuous, liquid lake practically thick enough to support her weight. But as she sank to her midriff in the ooze, she knew that she could not go on without flotation. She decided to build a raft.

Just as she used to make toy boats to sail imaginary explorers across the Citadel's fountain, she constructed a version that would keep her from sinking. She used logs instead of sticks, vine instead of thread; she had no cloth for a sail. When she was done, she had a makeshift raft that was long and narrow, one on which she could lie down and paddle on both sides.

She slogged slowly through the surface slime, parting the foliage with the raft's pointed prow, but leaving no wake: the vegetation closed in behind her without indication of her passage. The stump-filled bog soon yielded to a sparsely settled sea. Only an occasional leaf or piece of driftwood marred the tranquil surface. On

Entropy

and on she went, her imagination fired by what might lie before her; she was unable to rest. When the last pulpy stems were dragged off the woody extrusions of her raft, she found herself completely alone in an ocean devoid of life. Her innate sense of direction steered her course across the great unknown sea.

Her stamina waned, she became sluggish, and she could not rejuvenate her energy. At times she slumped on the lashed timbers in complete exhaustion, and drifted idly. Her mind wandered, then snapped back to renewed concentration; she must be prepared in case of attack from a submersible demon. But she encountered nothing more inimical than mild swells that imparted sickening motions to the raft.

Eons passed while she paddled and glided, paddled and glided, paddled and . . .

Sheena detected a change. The mist was every bit as thick, the sea just as expansive, the air as still; nevertheless, she sensed something tangible — something remarkable — beyond the veil of tranquility.

Then came the gentle lapping of waves against a granular beach, of fleeting whitecaps swallowed by the sand: no lush vegetation here, but a desert coastline that sloped moderately upward. When the lead log bumped against the bank, Sheena rolled off and waded ashore. She dragged the wooden raft out of the miniature surf.

She was overcome with relief at the sign of high ground devoid of thorny hedges, dense undergrowth, and forests thick with creeping vines. Quickly she ascended the tall barrier dunes until they plateaued high above the level of the sea. Nothing grew here, no animals lived. Sheena rested on a hilltop where she felt lighter and freer than she had in ages. Ever cautious, Sheena drew her sword and laid it down beside her.

Time passed. In a nearly somnambulant state she rose and retreated farther from the sea. The sand soon yielded to rocky outcrops that she climbed with pleasure. After the long strain of restricted motion during her oceanic crossing, the freedom of movement refreshed her. She stretched as she scaled pronounced promontories, delighting in the exercise that her body sorely needed. Soon she was higher than she had ever been in her life, higher even than the hallowed cupola that crowned the Citadel. She felt a strange lightness. Here she was surely above Council canon.

The fog was much thicker at altitude. The plateaus became shorter, the connecting pitches steeper. Sheena felt as if she were climbing right up into the sky. What awaited her in heaven?

Then came the tremor. It began as a barely discernible vibration welling out of the ground, progressed to a series of abrupt, uncontrolled jolts, and quickly reached the fury of a full-blown quake. Grains of sand bobbed in the air like dust, pebbles and small stones recoiled off the sharply shifting landmass.

Sheena's body was pulled apart by mysterious forces; she was pressed down against sharp crags that gouged her unmercifully. Awful waves of pressure undulated from high intensity to low. She understood none of what was happening, only that she was pinned in place and unable to move. No longer did loose debris bobble; now it was held to the ground by the same power that kept Sheena in its grip. She fought impending unconsciousness.

The pressure wave left as quickly as it had come. Stones stuck to vertical rock surfaces were released from their unnatural position, and fell down.

Sheena felt as if an omnipotent weight was suddenly lifted off every molecule of her being: her mind as well as her body seemed to hover giddily in space. Slowly she regained her senses. As she stretched to her full height, and worked aching muscles and stiffened joints, she felt herself continuing right on up, as if her mind were leaving her body and she could observe the cliff from afar.

Then she was seized with uncontrollable fear — for she was floating. The ledge was below her and out of reach. Her insides twisted painfully as she flailed in desperation and managed to grapple the vertical rock

Entropy

wall next to her. She pulled herself tight against the granular surface. Then she crept along the upright crags and crannies as if they were horizontal. What had been ledges were now overhangs. The escarpment was ninety degrees out of phase.

Sheena's mental disorientation continued as the world spun kaleidoscopically. Nausea dominated her faculties. She reached a juncture where two rock surfaces met at right angles; one plane was a shelf, but she no longer had any idea which way was down and which was out. She draped herself over the rim so when the topsy-turvy mountainside was restored to reality she could scramble to whichever plane became the bottom.

Sheena was afraid of falling off the edge of the world.

How long she clung to her precarious perch she did not know. Time itself ceased to pass. When awareness returned, Sheena found herself hanging half over the edge of a sheer cliff. She quickly edged away from the drop, but remained within reach in case physics took another turn for the absurd.

After a long while she reclaimed her wits, if not her composure. She vacillated between wanting to retreat down the mountain side to the beach and to the open reaches of the sea, where there existed a semblance of normalcy and familiarity, and forcing herself to go on into the unknown, perhaps into the unknowable.

Ultimately, she had no choice. To come this far and turn back admitted defeat and Sheena feared that more than she feared death.

She found herself on a barren plateau that stretched unobstructed to infinity. Mist hung in the air without the slightest motion, a permanent veil that grew thicker as Sheena penetrated farther into the nether regions. She skimmed across the gritty sandstone with effortless ease. The ground was a glidebelt as wide as the world.

Gradually, awareness of her surroundings dimmed. She could not focus her thoughts, or concentrate on her purpose.

Time slowed.

Sheena found herself in a dream world. The atmosphere was thick, syrupy. She moved only with the greatest effort, bound by ethereal reins. No longer did she know where she was, when she was, *if* she was. Her past was a patchwork montage no more real than the world around her. Her life might have been no more than an electronic pulse in the memory bank of a computer.

Space and time became meaningless equations.

Sheena thought she was about to die. Instead, she was reborn.

Chapter 7

"Over here! Quick!" Sheena dashed along the edge of the wall, following her sword.

Marek was right behind her. "What is it?"

Although the highway terminated at the metal barrier, an intersecting offshoot veered to one side into a broad passageway. In the maintenance space beneath the roadbed an ebony carpet undulated, and oily globules roiled.

"You do not want to know."

Sheena raced up the ramp as a drooling sphere separated from the writhing mass and launched itself into the air. After a short parabolic curve, the black blob smacked onto the ramp. Thick, unctuous liquid splashed outward concentrically from the impact area.

"You are right." Nevertheless, Marek was soon to learn.

The amorphous glob contracted into a ball and rolled after them. Another sphere exploded from the black mass and plopped down next to the first. Then came another, and another, and another. Soon the ramp was saturated with slime. Each blob pulled itself together with a life of its own.

The ramp leveled out onto a platform in a courtyard-sized chamber the farthest side of which was a heavily armored bulkhead from which bulged a series of rectangular coamings and huge metal hatchways. Flanking the closed gates at either end were large, open booths. Parked inside were wheeled vehicles similar to those in Erbridge used to transport tools and construction equipment. Electrical recharging cables dangled out of wall sockets.

Marek spun into a defense position, pike outstretched. "What now?"

Sheena raced for a control panel between two coamings. "If we can get this hatch open — "

"What about *them*?"

"Just hold them off. You cannot kill them."

"What do you mean by — "

Then the first one was upon him. Marek slashed downward with the axe-blade of his pike and perfectly bisected the oncoming blob. Carried along by forward momentum, the two halves skittered away in diverging directions. The steel blade gouged into the lead-lined floor, and stuck. Marek yanked it loose just in time to stab the next blob with the tip, pinning it. As he withdrew his weapon from the yielding flesh the gash filled in, like two bowls of soft jelly.

"What *are* these things?"

Sheena struggled with the cranking mechanism. "Pure protoplasm."

Since the thing would not die, Marek batted it with the flat of his pike and knocked it halfway across the room.

"Keep chopping them apart. The fragments need time to recuperate. And at all costs, do not let them touch you."

Marek slashed from side to side as the blobs tried to roll into him. Those he struck broadside spun away and were momentarily disoriented. The ones he cleaved in two rolled about until they either reformed into smaller balls, or until the pieces bumped into another piece — not necessarily from its original unity — and fused into a new whole.

"The gears are rusted! I need help — "

Marek scooped a protoplasmic blob onto the end of his pike and pitched it hard against the far wall. He scythed the next three into fractions. During the lull before the next horde arrived, he joined Sheena in the alcove.

"You are stronger — " She indicated the protruding handles.

Marek brushed her aside and studied the electrical panel. "There is still emergency power." He punched a button that initiated a batch of alarms. "And a pressure differential." The annunciator board indicated the problem. "I have to shunt the ancillary circuits — "

Entropy

"Do it!" Sheena ducked under his pike and slashed her blade through the oncoming blobs. The air was thick with oily residue as she tore them apart with rapid dispatch. The floor was soon paved with slime that quivered gruesomely as it coagulated into homogenous substances.

Marek opened the cabinet door, identified the override terminals, and shunted power with jumper wires provided for emergency situations. The two massive hatches on either side separated from the floor and slid into hidden recesses above. The screech of metal grinding on ungreased runners was accompanied by a terrible, roaring hiss.

He yanked Sheena back into the alcove between the coamings. "The other side is evacuated!"

A tremendous wind raked across the chamber into the void under the hatches. Dust and loose debris were scooped up in a brown cloud and swept across the room with the force of a tornado. Living protoplasm resisted the slipstream by flattening against the floor; but soon the torrent of air was too much for it. The smaller blobs were peeled off the smooth lead and sucked into the twin voids.

As the hatches rose higher, the eddy currents grew stronger. Black blobs of protoplasm whipped past them at ever-increasing speeds. Those that rolled into the far side of the chamber continued their madcap flight straight out the hatches. Soon their numbers thinned. Then, only an occasional amorphous sphere dared enter the room.

Marek pulled off the jumpers. With the mechanism no longer bypassed, the hatches stopped ascending. Pressure sensitive switches took control. The lifting motors were idled, the clamping devices released, and the hatches slammed down hard into the grooved track. The awful tempest ceased instantly.

Marek relaxed his grip.

Slipping free from his hold, Sheena rushed across the chamber toward the revetments. "Hurry! We must get out before the next wave arrives. Once it senses life, it will stop at nothing."

With hardly enough time to gather his wits, Marek followed her lead.

Sheena squeezed between a vehicle and the adjacent partition. "The sectioned cars conveyed people, the larger ones carried bulk freight," she explained hastily, as she grappled with the lifting apparatus knobs. "If we can get this hatch open — "

Marek paused to inspect the machine. He craned into the cab and fiddled with the switches. The engine hummed into life.

Startled, Sheena spun around with sword extended, and poised to defend or attack. "How — how did you do that?"

"I switched on the energy cell." Abandoning his long-shafted pike, Marek climbed into the operator's compartment and studied the gauges. "The battery is weak and the charging circuit is dead. It will not take us far, but if you open the gate, I will drive us through."

Now it was Sheena's turn to do as told. She cranked the wheel that lifted the door. Since the hatch was not heavily armored like those that opened the way into the next highway compartment, she had the strength to raise it. There was only slight pressure equalization.

She waved him through even before the hatch was all the way up. "Come on."

Marek engaged the drive train. Wheels that had not moved in ages refused to budge. He applied more power. The transmission suddenly took hold and banged into gear. The truck lurched forward. "Climb aboard."

Sheena pulled the emergency drop lever. The hatch fell with a crash, but not before half a dozen globules darted through the opening. One blob was crushed by the weight of the hatch; the undamaged portion tore itself free and sculpted its remaining matter into a tiny sphere.

Sheena jumped into the cab and slammed the door behind her. "Get going, before it finds a way inside." The blobs attached themselves to the chassis and worked their way up the fenders. "It is attracted to life like iron to a magnet."

The truck crunched through gravel and broken crystals littering the pavement; chipped facets in the ceiling refracted its passage. Extruded protoplasm squeezed through shaft glands. Sheena sheered off tiny globules as soon as they appeared.

"You keep saying 'it,' yet there are scores of them. Hundreds."

"It is one collective organism. Various divisions thrive in some of the other abandoned lower levels, the same as this one." She flattened another extrusion with the edge of her sword, and stabbed the other loose blobs in the cab while they were still disoriented. "It is a primitive protoplasmic life form with the ability to divide into components each with the instinct of the whole. The parts recombine with the larger entity when they have completed their task."

"Which is?"

"To bring more life." Sheena pointed to an inscription on the wall. "The 'up' ramp is that way. We have a choice of continuing underground or going back to the surface. Which do you prefer?"

"The fire of demons weighs less heavily upon my mind than the mindless vermin of these subterranean passageways."

"A wise expression."

"A logical conclusion."

"As you will." Sheena lopped off another blob and bounced it into a corner. It huddled uncomfortably close in the confines of the cab. "But first we must get rid of this parasite."

Marek steered the truck up the ramp. "How?"

Sheena opened the door and chopped in half the blob clinging to the rim. She scraped off each part with her blade. The two halves pirouetted dizzyingly in nearly parallel paths, then splatted together and began to reorganize. "Can this truck go any faster?"

"Not without pushing."

Another blob crept along the side of the cab, leaving

an oily residue on the plastic panel. A slender pseudo-pod protruded from the central mass and waved in Sheena's direction. "Mindless it may be, but its will to survive is phenomenal." Viciously she hacked it into little pieces. "We must abandon the truck."

Marek eased off the power.

"At full speed," Sheena added hastily. "As we approach the topside airlock."

Marek shoved the throttle against the peg. "You seem to know exactly where we are going."

"All the castles are built alike. The differences between them are artistic rather than functional. Underground thoroughfares are separated into airtight vaults with double-chambered access."

"Why?"

"Ask the Ancients."

"I hope never to meet one."

"I doubt if you will. Only their legacy survives them, and most of that is lost in forgotten computer codes."

"Wilam was deciphering — "

"This is where we get out." Sheena sheathed her sword, and pointed. "Can you aim the truck past that hatch so it will collide against the far wall?"

"If you wish, although I hate to destroy a working model. Not that many remain."

"Better a truck than the world of which it is a part."

Marek turned the wheel that controlled the rear axle. The truck veered onto a new course so close to the adjacent wall that the open door scraped against it.

"Far enough away so we do not get killed making our escape." Marek changed the angle slightly. "I am right behind you."

Sheena leaped out as the truck approached the hatch coaming. She hit the deck and rolled. Marek was right behind her. By the time he regained his poise, Sheena had the hatch cranked halfway open — enough for them to duck under.

Two blobs detached from the truck just before it slammed into the shiny metal wall and was demolished. Another blob rolled up the ramp and over the

Entropy

short sill.

"Quick! Get it down!"

Marek spun the crank assembly, sealing the hatch before the other two blobs were even close. "One got through!"

Sheena slammed the side of her sword hard against the viscous, jellylike ball. It flattened against the floor like a black puddle. She then quartered it quickly, and scattered the pieces with four deft sideswipes. "It will be senseless for a moment." Then she was off.

Marek raced after her. A fine mist sprinkled the garage with slender gray filaments. Outside, a flock of flapping creatures flew out of the trees. Ground varmints shuffled along unafraid of the intruders. The pavement was cracked and overgrown with grass. Ornate walls once tall and proud lay in ruins across a courtyard fountain, while fallen statues struck poses of the dead.

One of the protoplasm fragments rolled unerringly toward an unsuspecting varmint. The blob hit the creature with a splash. Black, unctuous oil spread over the animal before it had a chance to mobilize a defense; within moments it was completely enveloped. The animal bounded away wearing a coat of protoplasm, but did not go far before keeling over. For a long time it continued to struggle inside the black cocoon, as if it had changed one skin for another.

Soon it only twitched. Then it lay still.

"Eventually, the protoplasm will absorb the tissue completely."

Marek was aghast. "Should we not — try to — kill it? Before it spreads?"

"The demons will do that for us. It is their job."

Chapter 8
Flashback

Marek made the final adjustment to the motor. With the power leads insulated and bolted tight to the terminal blocks, all it needed was a surge of electricity to begin rotation. He clamped the inspection plate over the maintenance port.

"Just like new," he declared proudly.

"As it must be. With no replacements available and spare parts scarce, we must salvage every machine, instrument, and electronic component we possess." Tomas slipped into the operator's cab and switched on the grid. "It is powering up smoothly." He scrutinized the gauges. "No immediate short circuits. Climb aboard, and we will go for a test drive."

Even though Marek knew his work was good, he felt a twinge of doubt. "We could block the wheels and check the drive train under increasing load."

"Son, you need less caution and more self-confidence." The motor hummed as Tomas advanced the throttle. "For one so young you show good sense. And your mechanical skill is extraordinary. But you must learn that a machine is more than gears and shafts and bits of wire, more than an assembly of sub-units. Its ultimate usefulness lies not in the performance of its individual parts, but in its ability to function as a whole."

Marek got into the cab repeating the catechism in his mind: a machinist makes parts, an engineer assembles them and creates something useful. "I just thought — "

"Quite all right, son. Quite all right." The car moved along slowly, evenly. Tomas drove out of the garage and into the lot where disabled vehicles awaited repair. A thin mist clung to the treetops. "There is enough work here to keep you occupied for a lifetime — but you have a larger calling."

Entropy

"Father, please — "

"You must pay attention. It is for your own good. And since you will soon be apprenticed, I have much to explain."

"But Father — "

"The castle is a cruel place, ruled by cruel leaders. In order to survive in this world you need to win favor with those in power."

"Is that why you have apprenticed me to guard school?" Marek regretted the remark as soon as it was made. "I did not mean — "

"Never mind, son. I understand your consternation. It must seem a terrible treachery to have your own father turn you over to Council prerogative. That is why I must show you certain things."

Tomas turned into a lane where a construction crew was repairing a rift in the road. Guards in work habiliments wielded whips upon workers not performing to satisfaction. Pain and anguish were evident. As hard as the laborers toiled, the guards demanded more.

"There is great disparity between the classes. Council members and their attendants live in the highest quarters, while we subsist in the lowest tenements. They dally in the pleasures of the flesh, while we slave to keep the castle from falling apart. They have privileges that we do not, and they give orders that we must obey."

"Then why give in to their evildoing?" Marek protested vehemently. "Why not contest that which is wrong?"

"There are many ways of fighting, Son. Open rebellion often fails where subtle crusade conquers. Many people have been slain outright for opposing Council authority. Experience has shown that diplomacy without might is ineffectual."

Marek mused long and hard.

Tomas took a byway that wound through open woodlands, in some places abutting the castle rampart. Atop the high parapet sentries kept their lonely vigil. They had been guarding the stone walls for so long that no one knew anymore what they were guarding against. Yet, the thoughtless surveillance continued: that was the way it always had been, and the way the Council wanted it always to be.

"Is there a better way?"

Tomas drove leisurely through the castle confines, past fields of grass and hillocks of rock, on raised roadways over low-lying swamp, by rural work camps, disused lodgings, and fallen buildings. Marek never realized how much land the castle enclosed. His childhood had been spent in close proximity to the Citadel, the center of activity and civilization, such as it was.

He was well aware of the continuing downfall of technology. As a special projects engineer, his father complained bitterly about the constant decline in the maintenance and repair of essential appliances, the loss of competent help, the cutbacks in education, and increasing Council decadence. This trip through the outback demonstrated even more the perdition of Erbridge, made evident by overt ruin and desolation, loss and abandonment.

"There is a different way."

Tomas stopped the car in front of a huge pound full of worn-out machines and broken-down vehicles. Grass grew tall through the cracked pavement, thick vines covered the dilapidated fence, and shrubbery sprouted through many of the disjointed chassis. The rear wall of the closure was the inner rampart, itself caving in, a mound of debris at its base. No sentinels patrolled this part of the castle so far from the lofty Citadel.

Marek did not recognize any of the strange contrivances rusting away, forsaken. "What is this place?"

"A repository for equipment beyond repair, or for which we no longer have any use, or whose purpose is forgotten. It is a junkyard depicting Erbridge's past glory. It is a warning."

After a moment of reflection, Tomas put the car in gear and accelerated away from the mechanical scrap heap. The way back to the Citadel was long and circuitous, the land largely unoccupied. Marek had time to wonder: if out here was untamed territory, what existed beyond the castle walls?

At the base of the Citadel, Tomas took a ramp down to the lower level. A group of women scrubbed dirt and grime off the tunnel walls, and polished the facets of the crystal facade; areas frequented by Council members were kept meticulously clean. From basement to sub-basement to sub-sub-basement, the little car purred.

"Where are we going now?"

"To the source of power."

"Is that not at the top of the Citadel, where the Council sits in chamber?"

"No. That is where the power is used. The fountain of origin is deep underground. While you are still in my charge, I want to show it to you — so you will understand what we are up against."

Tomas steered the car into a mammoth cavern whose walls glittered vibrantly, whose smooth floor thrummed. He parked at the base of a towering monolith that throbbed with potent energy. Heavily insulated bus bars the size of tree trunks vaulted through the top of the domed ceiling. To his very core, Marek could feel the tremendous electrical potential crackling in the air, creeping along his body.

"Do not worry," Tomas cautioned. "It is not dangerous."

Marek was overawed. "Is this a — transformer?"

"Not just any transformer, but *the* transformer: the main power converter for the entire castle. Through its windings have gone all the electricity Erbridge has ever used." Tomas left the car and approached the monolith with the solemnity of a man approaching god. "Have you ever wondered where electricity originates?"

Marek got out of the car, but remained reverently by its side. The depth of the cavern was oppressive. "It is drawn from the ground."

"The schoolroom answer. Do you know how it gets into the ground in the first place?"

Marek was nonplussed. "I — I have never thought about it." Slowly, falteringly, he followed his father's meandering. Only when the two paused side by side did Marek's towering stature become apparent. "Magnetism generates electricity." He could feel the flux through the lead-lined floor. "Is there magnetic induction deep beneath the surface?"

"A brilliant inference, considering your state of knowledge. You have not disappointed me."

Marek felt as if he had passed some kind of test, an intellectual rite of passage.

"But your answer merely begs another question: what generates magnetism? These devices here — " Tomas indicated the massive units surrounding the transformer. " — are merely collectors, the perceptible portions of enormous devices designed and built by the Ancients. They understood the workings, they understood the physical principals involved. But I do not — nor does anyone else alive."

"Do you mean that we do not generate the electricity ourselves?"

"That is what I mean. The Ancients tapped into a long-lasting underground source of energy, the knowledge of which is buried with it. The induction devices furnish the raw power to these collectors, which then send the wild current to the transformer for conversion to usable energy. All we control is the output."

Marek studied the colossal machinery that filled a cavern into which the Citadel could be placed in its entirety and lost in perspective. The scale was an order of magnitude larger than anything he had ever known. Yet the implications of the lost science on which the power supply was based was more stunning than the size of the apparatus.

"I cannot imagine . . . "

"Nor can I," Tomas agreed. "Trying to conceive what incredible forces flow beneath us is like fathoming what lies on the other side of the wall at the end of the world. It is all a great mystery."

As father and son beheld the awesome power before

them, and contemplated the tremendous forces of nature that induced it, an ornate, gilded limousine entered the cavern. It stopped next to the plain utility vehicle Tomas had been driving. When the cloaked Council member emerged, he signaled for his chauffeur to wait.

Marek suddenly felt more apprehension about the power wielded by this mortal than about the unknown energy source of the Ancients.

"Do you still instruct the boy in engineering theory?" The lack of formal address was purposely impertinent.

Tomas did not let it bother him. "Charel, in the time we have remaining together, I thought it wise that he procure a broad basis of understanding about how this world of ours operates. It may help him later in life."

Charel made no notice of the stress on "ours." "Palace guards have no need of such knowledge. They require only large and well-muscled bodies. We will teach him the discipline and arcane skills necessary for his new post: combat, weaponry, adroitness. If he does well, he may rise above the level of retainer."

"Marek is a quick learner. I am certain he will advance rapidly through the ranks."

"Rest assured that he will have my personal guidance."

"I thank you for that, Charel. May I also count on your support with regard to matters of maintenance?" Before the Council member could respond, Tomas hurried on, "Recent power surges have burnt out some of the collectors. Since this has never happened before, no one knows how to repair them. I — "

"You are the chief engineer. The Council relies on your expertise in such matters. You need no support other than that which has already been assigned. If the job is too big for you, perhaps we should consider a replacement."

Tomas ignored the rebuke. "Perhaps you misunderstood. *No* one knows how to effect the necessary repairs. There are no records, nor has anyone ever disassembled a collector to learn the intricacies of its construction and operation. Lately, induction ratios have been so erratic that I fear for the safety of the converter. If its windings should be damaged, Erbridge could lose all power."

Charel rankled. "You suggest I authorize transgression into the realm of the Ancients. Such insolence borders on heresy. Sheena was banished for her unorthodox views, as her mother was before her. Pray that you do not fall into the same category."

During the diatribe, Marek was ignored; he was a spectator to issues he knew nothing about and could barely follow. But his notions about his father's impuissance quickly changed to newfound admiration.

"Again you misunderstand me. Recapturing the forgotten science of our progenitors is vitally important to our survival — "

"Now you cross the border with open impiety. The Ancients were not our ancestors, but our creators. And their science is not forgotten, it is forbidden. They placed us upon this world for a purpose that is divine and therefore beyond our comprehension. Those who meddle with proscription are the ones responsible for provoking the wrath that will destroy us all. Do I make myself clear?"

Tomas paused long before answering. "Quite clear."

"Then leave this place at once." Charel turned his back and started off.

"I will leave my guard to ensure your compliance." As he entered the limousine, he signaled for his personal bodyguard to remain. Then Charel was gone. The man left behind made Marek look small; he rippled his armor with the hilt of his sword.

Tomas led Marek to the car. "Now you know what we are up against. We are not fighting ignorance alone, but intentional disregard. The Council is deathly afraid that any change in the status quo will result in their loss of power. They alter the truth to fit their notion of what they would like it to be. What they fail to realize is that the real power of the world lies here; that each nonworking collector shuts down another power grid."

Marek got into the car. "Is that why the far end of the castle has become nonfunctional?"

"Yes. And as these uncontrollable power surges increase in intensity, more damage will occur. Charel can blame me if he chooses, but that will not restore the power once it is lost. Council mandates cannot reestablish magnetic flux."

Tomas started the motor and eased on the throttle. The car pulled away, leaving Charel's guard alone in the vast cavern, dwarfed by the machines of the Ancients.

"I am afraid, Father. I hate the Council, and Charel especially. They are bad individuals, and command their guards to carry out despicable deeds." Marek was aghast. "What if I am ordered to — hurt people?"

"Sometimes we do what we must, not what we want."

Marek was in turmoil. His size belied his age; he was still a child with childish notions. "I could not possibly hurt anyone, Father, no matter what the consequences."

Tomas pampered his son's immaturity. "I trust your conscience to guide you. Plus, you will have help. There is one among the Council who is different from the rest. He is good, and he recognizes the slender thread by which Erbridge hangs. His name is Wilam. He will protect you; he will be your tutor."

Chapter 9

The Council chamber was empty. The citadel was abandoned. The ramparts were cracked and crumbling, and in many places completely broken down. No one lived here.

With the entire castle at their disposal, Sheena and Marek rested from their ordeal in the highest Council quarters. Although ransacked and extensively damaged, the luxurious appointments still exuded a royal splendor. Platinum hangings, bronze statuary, detailed dioramas, and exquisite works of art embellished the apartments of once-proud masters. But the hallowed galleries that once exhibited the glory of an exalted race now served as little more than epitaphs.

"I never fully appreciated how relaxing these lofty levels could be." Marek stretched tired muscles, and exercised with his newfound sword. "I feel more comfortable with a blade."

"You have your choice of weapons. The arsenal is yours for the taking." Sheena turned on electrical switches and was surprised to find partial power flowing through the circuits. "Even without maintenance, the work of the Ancients endures. I wonder how long it has been since these people became extinct."

"I noticed several desiccated bodies lying in the lower chambers, making it appear that the last hangers-on died not long ago."

"What kind of clothes were they wearing?"

"Commoner's. There was no sign of aristocracy."

Sheena contemplated the significance of that. "Marek, do you think you can get into the computer and dig out a few facts?"

"I can try." He attached the input probes to various parts of his body, the same way he had done many times working with Wilam. The wire insulation was thin in spots, and some of the contacts were fouled. "The processing unit is intact but most of the sensors are

Entropy   61

nonfunctional. I cannot reach the memory chips. With enough time I might be able to rig a bypass — "

"No. Do not bother. I was just curious." Sheena wandered across the room, examining other items of equipment. "We are sliding backward, and the world is winding down. What happened here is what will happen to all of us if we do not do something about it. Our quest for the Sacred Portal takes precedence over idle interest. Let us be on our way."

Sheena left the room and descended the broad ramp that spiraled down the inside of the citadel.

Marek ripped off the electrodes and chased after her. "You are surely driven, Sheena."

"Time is essential. Gigantic forces are tearing the world apart. Your father told you that; and my father, too. The castle ramparts were designed to protect us from harm, but we are being attacked in ways that render such fortifications useless. The constant disturbances of the ground, the irregular deviation of magnetic flux — these are worldwide forces."

"And the wall at the end of the world? According to legend it was erected to keep out evil forces. Why is it not working? If it really exists — "

"You doubt me?" Sheena expressed more hurt than anger.

Marek was quick to explain. "I do not doubt *you*, only what you think you encountered. Slipping in and out of consciousness — "

Torn silver drapes hung over the burnished banister. The facade on the outer turn of the ramp was peeling off its mounts. The ramp itself was no longer smooth, but rippled; the citadel's foundations had been displaced vertically by a major quake.

"I know it appears there were lapses in my memory — lost time for which I cannot account. But the wall was there. It exists. I did not imagine it."

"*Something* is there. Not a wall the way we think of it, but some kind of intangible barrier." Marek reached the ground floor of the citadel and preceded Sheena across cracked, upthrust marble. "Something that is beyond *my* imagination to comprehend." Marek stopped in the mist-laden courtyard, overgrown with wild grass and climbing vines. "It is too much for me to accept. First I am ordered outside the castle ramparts, whose passage has been denied in all of recorded history. Then you describe a mystical barricade which for some reason is impassible. And what lies beyond that? Another wall? Then another? And another? Where does it all end?"

"Where does infinity end? For that matter, where does infinity begin?"

"Now you take after your father. He was always spouting riddles in the form of aphorisms."

"Then I will be more specific. Suppose the truth behind the legends of the wall at the end of the world has been reversed? Suppose the purpose of that wall was not to keep evil forces out, but to keep us in?"

Bewildered, Marek halted at the side of the dry fountain.

Sheena paused long enough to confront Marek with her convictions. "You have spent your entire life within the confines of the castle, secure in the knowledge that the world existed the way you perceived it. But now you know that the world is a far different place from that portrayed in school. Demons are mechanical constructs programmed with specific instructions. Animals that rove the swamps and forests are not only unknown to us, many of them are alien life forms that do not conform to our biological type. The world is subject to tectonic principals that do not conform to the laws of physics. None of these things makes sense; added together they become an irrational whole. Come. We must be on our way."

Again, Marek was forced to chase after her. At the edge of the courtyard, they passed a long-dead body huddled against the gate. The flesh was almost completely decomposed; the rotted robe covering the armor identified it as the remains of a palace guard.

"All of that is true. I helped design and build many instruments and scientific measuring devices for your

Entropy

father, and I worked closely with him in recording their results. But I seldom knew what the experiments proved, and never understood his interpretations. If only we could have had more time together — "

Sheena displayed less emotion than she felt. "You must put him out of your mind, as I have done. He no longer exists. Remember him not for who he was to you, but what he stood for."

Marek matched her speed. "Oh, but he does exist. He will always exist." He tapped the supply satchel that held the computer crystal. "In memory."

"Perhaps."

"And perhaps he is better off now than when he was alive in that pain-wracked body. He suffered so much at the end that he could not think properly. He babbled nonsense. He — " Marek halted. "I — I am sorry. I — "

"Never mind. We can honor him best by completing his work. By dispelling the mystery with which our world is clouded. By learning what he meant by the secret of the stars. What *are* stars?"

"Concentrations of matter and energy that emit radiation and exert force at a distance."

"But what does that mean? And why are they important?"

"Wilam concluded that because of the way our world is enclosed, they are not directly observable. He had information on them only from the data banks."

"And how can the world possibly have a wall — " Sheena's uncanny senses detected an enemy presence.

Marek drew his sword. "What is it — ?"

"There." Lurking in the castle's overgrown park were distinctly clothed males with evil intent. "Erbridge palace guards."

"How did they find us?"

"Of more immediate import is why they do not attack."

"They fear the fate of Boram. Perhaps they wait for greater numbers." Sheena left her sword untouched. "Then let us leave in haste."

They rushed away in the opposite direction, but the

palace guards, huddled in hiding, erupted from cover and charged after them. There were half a dozen, and they were heavily armed and armored. None advanced before the others; they maintained an even line and kept a safe distance.

Marek pulled Sheena to a halt. "It is an ambush. They use the same tactics against rioting citizens."

Sheena quickly assessed the situation. "What do you suggest we do?"

Marek was taken aback. "I thought *you* gave the orders."

"You know their methods. Take the lead."

Marek studied the lay of the land, the density of the trees in the park, the thick brush that clogged the streets, the tall piles of rubble that were once outbuildings. "If we take a ninety degree turn we can outflank them. And the more open space, the better." Yet he did not move.

"So be it." Sheena chose the direction, and started out at full speed across the broken pavement. She nimbly climbed a pile of debris to the roof of a low structure. "You were right. They are on to our ruse and seek to cut us off."

Marek, twice her size and very agile, nearly overtook her. "We will be hard pressed if it comes to personal combat."

"In that I disagree. But let us flee if we can, to reduce the bloodshed." She leaped to an adjacent roof that was still partially intact. "There is no sense killing those we can outwit."

Marek landed by her side. Their combined weight fractured the tile and snapped the support beam. Both of them tumbled into the room below. Neither was hurt, but they fell among machinery and landscaping tools that crammed the shed to capacity. By the time they disentangled themselves and reached the narrow doorway, the main patrol was passing along both sides of the building, and one guard blocked the path of retreat with his sword.

Sheena whipped out her sword with resignation.

Entropy

"Now we are forced to fight." The shiny steel blade was honed to razor sharpness: if laid upon flesh, its weight alone was enough to make it slide through skin, sever sinew, and flay muscle. Only a slight pressure need be added to puncture armor.

She lunged at the guard towering above her, undismayed at his size. He parried left, then parried right, with more expertise than Sheena expected. But when she feinted a move, he swung wildly to ward off the blow. She stabbed her sword straight into his body, pulled out her blade, and turned so fast toward the next opponent that the dead guard had not yet fallen before she dispatched the other.

"Fight!"

Marek took a protective stance. He held off three guards at once.

Sheena shoved him from behind. "Take the offensive!" She spun on an attacker plunging forward with a lance. Her controlled swing lopped off the barbed tip, but she took the blunted shaft in the midriff. The momentum knocked her down. She railed out from under, sliced upward, and disemboweled her antagonist.

Marek backed down as all three guards pushed against him at the same time. His blade was bloodless, but it carved the air with a speed that hypnotized the trio and kept them at bay. Sheena waded into the battle and engaged the guard on the left. Against only two guards, Marek was evenly matched. With firm, directed strokes, he pointed and parried, pointed and parried, until he found an opening. His blade bit through armor and disgorged blood, nearly cleaving the body in two. He ran the other one through in a vicious frontal assault; his blade pierced armor and continued to penetrate until checked by the hilt.

Sheena drove in like a whirlwind. The guard fought valiantly, but once put on the defensive could do nothing but retreat. She feinted, slashed downward, and carved off a sizable chunk of her adversary's side. Armor plates peeled off, flesh and organs spattered onto the ground. The guard was still reeling when Sheena commanded, "Come on!"

Unable to retrieve his blade, Marek swiped one from a vanquished foe. "More are coming." He bowled over small shrubs in anxious retreat.

Sheena weaved through hedgerows, saplings, and piles of debris. Nothing slowed her pace. The decrepit castle environs were more of a deferent to nervous palace guards now deliberately lethargic.

Long fissures split the castle grounds in the pattern of cracked mud at the bottom of a dry creek. Sheena and Marek hopped the crustal fractures in zigzag fashion. Often, no bottom was discernible. Most of the rampart had been destroyed by ground tremors. Sheena raced through a building-sized break in the wall and across the moat that was partially filled with collapsed stonework. She easily climbed up the opposite side, then turned to wait for Marek.

"Sheath your sword."

Marek followed her example, then scaled the uneven side of the moat. "They lag behind."

"I do not think they will come after us for a while, at least until they regroup."

"More than that. The officers will re-evaluate the situation before they place more men at risk. That is the way they retreated from pitched battles at home."

Sheena was awe-struck. "Battles? What battles?"

"You have been away too long. Erbridge is in revolution. Only because the citizens are unarmed, and fight with makeshift weapons, are they held in subjugation. I thought you knew that."

"I had only a short time in the castle before I was forced to flee for my life. Long enough to tell Father about my circumscription — " Sheena's thoughts flashed back to those final few moments. It pained her to dwell on her father's condition. "Let us move on, lest we be forced to kill more of those whose lives we are trying to save."

In a short time they found themselves deep in the swamp, with no signs of pursuit. They splashed

Entropy

through shallow pools thick with ichor, and waded through rank miasma that Sheena hoped the palace guards would fear to roam.

"They are trained well in the use of weapons, but are still innocent of the perils of the wild. I pity them the horrors they have yet to encounter."

"Quite a compliment coming from one who bested them so easily," Marek allowed. "But I agree about the perils. The unknown frightens me more than meeting an enemy in combat — even if I did falter when — "

"Forget it, Marek. And forgive yourself. I found death just as difficult to mete the first time I crossed swords."

Marek showed confusion. "Sheena, I thought — that is, I — I could have gotten us killed. I did not obey you quickly enough, and your prophecy nearly came true."

Sheena was stoical. "You survived and, hopefully, you have learned my reason for sternness."

"I appreciate that now more than ever. Furthermore, I — I am surprised at your leniency."

In many ways Marek exhibited boyish traits that Sheena found refreshing. His naivety contrasted sharply with his moments of maturity. "You did well back there. You have strength without ruthlessness. I would trust less one too eager to kill."

The swamp gave rise to higher ground covered with brush through which a twin track passed. Sheena indicated the telltale grooves. "The route of a demon."

Marek reached for his sword. "Should we be on our guard?"

"We should always be on our guard. In this case, perhaps more against what it stalks. There are animals in the wilderness that fit into a scheme of life in which we are out of place. Some of these animals are large, and kill. I did not mention this before because I did not want to frighten you right off."

"Why? What does it all mean?"

"It means," Sheena alleged resolutely, "that this is not our world. We did not evolve here."

Chapter 10
Flashback

Tremulously, Wilam pushed himself away from the computer console. Every movement induced pain, every passing moment brought more suffering. "I am at a loss to explain your strange case of delirium, Baby. Patients with fevers often lose control of their senses, their minds. They may even hallucinate. But I cannot equate sickness to your experience. I know you were exhausted, perhaps overwrought, but you are too sensible a person to be deceived by stress."

Sheena found the chamber confining. She had been gone a long time, and had spent most of that time in the open. She loved exploring, roaming free in a land unknown — and reducing that unknown to the familiar. But she was also a physical person, enjoying the challenge to her body that travel produced. That made her much more aware of her father's debilitating condition.

"The world is truly a strange place — stranger than I imagined in my wildest dreams." Wilam shuffled with exaggerated motion that did not fully disguise his cramps and twinges. "All my life I have wondered what was out there, beyond the castle rampart — but another rampart? And so long that you cannot find a way around it? Reality is indeed more mysterious than myth."

"Deadlier, too." Sheena's armor was singed from a demon's blast.

"In more ways than one. The injuries to your person only hint at the havoc these so-called myths may inflict upon the world."

Wilam wandered off into his own world — an intellectual world. He was still for so long that Sheena feared some mental incapacitation. Her father had always been eccentric, but he began acting more odd than ever since her return — since she gave him the

Entropy

details of her journey.

"Father?"

Wilam shook himself from his reverie. "Yes, Baby. Sorry. I was wondering. This bulwark you encountered — it — it intrigues me. It fascinates me. It is no simple phenomenon. Once I accept the observable evidence, it overthrows the most deep-rooted barrier of all — the psychological barrier: that of the finite mind attempting to grasp the infinite. This impalpable barrier at the end of the world — if indeed it *is* the end of the world — must be a force field generated by an enormous energy source."

"Natural? Constructed by the Ancients? Or by someone else?"

"Good questions all, with answers for none. In one momentous stroke, you have dashed to pieces all the accepted notions of recorded history. You have placed in doubt the fable of our origin — which, I might add, will have a decided effect upon the hierarchy of civilization. The Council will not accept so easily facts that might topple hereditary dominance."

Sheena's dramatic return had been met with open hostility from Council members, who understood at once the significance of her findings if not the scientific meaning. Already there were grumblings throughout the populace that understood neither; her reappearance was little less than prophetic. Sheena had followed the path of her mother. But unlike her mother, she had returned with tales of far-off lands and free-born people.

But this was peripheral to Sheena's intent. The sad state of local affairs was insignificant when weighed against the greater consequences of her discoveries. And any space she had remaining for feelings was reserved for her father. When she departed on her journey, Wilam's condition was declining: he complained of aches and physical debility, and infirmity increasing with the passage of time. Now, after her long absence, he shocked her with a body wizened with age and trembling with pain.

"Forget the Council. What about the toppling of the world? Everywhere I go there are tremendous quakes, and incredible pressure waves that knock everything down, and huge cracks that suck the very air into the ground, and horrible animals, and mechanical demons. Death and destruction are everywhere — "

Sheena was interrupted by the door alarm. To save her father's strength, she hastened into the antechamber and answered the call herself. The man waiting impatiently wore the robes of an apprentice provost.

"I am Boram." He did not need to mention his station.

Sheena recognized him with great misgivings. "I know you." She was careful to keep her distance as she let him enter the room.

"I thought you might, Sheena. You have matured nicely since we last played together. You are beautiful."

"We never played. We fought. And if your manners have not improved, we are bound to fight again."

Boram put on a show of innocence. "We were in our youth then. Now we are adults."

"If you act as an adult, I will treat you as such. But do not attempt to seduce me again or I will retaliate in ways unknown to me as a girl."

Boram maintained his poise as he searched for a reply. "Did you acquire such venom on your travels, or has it burned within you always?"

"It makes no difference, as long as you understand that it is not misdirected."

Boram's attempt at dignified indifference fell flat. "Very well. As long as *you* understand that *I* will become a Council member. I prefer to have you *by* my side rather than against it."

"We all have our preferences." Sheena dismissed him with her back, and did not bother to invite him in.

Boram followed her on his own account. "Wilam, I trust you are in good health."

"Why the sudden interest in my well-being?"

"Why are these chambers filled with hostility?"

"It is typical of you to answer a question with a

Entropy 71

question, but I will not be so devious: it is because such hostility is justly deserved. And let us remember that being Charel's son does not entitle you to harass either my daughter or me. I am a Council member, you are merely a messenger boy for your father: an apprentice with ambitions. What business do you have with me?"

Boram was quite taken aback. His response was slow in coming. "You would do well not to — "

"Do not threaten me. It is I, after all, who have the authority to have you removed from my quarters. The palace guards still respond to my bidding. Just get down to business."

Boram was deflated. "Very well. I bring demands from the Council. You are to cease immediately your sacrilegious investigations, your scientific experimentation, and your illegal use of the computer."

"And for that you expected me to be hospitable? You are more than a fool, you are an idiot. Get out of my presence before I have you escorted out." When Boram did not move quickly enough, Wilam shoved him with the little strength his body retained. "Out. Get out. And next time, ask Charel to have the courage and the courtesy to deliver his own ultimatums. He may have influence with the Council, but he does not yet dominate it."

"You will pay — "

"Get out!" Wilam's rebuke was followed by physical assault. The blows did not hurt the apprentice provost's brawny body, but the psychic impact was devastating to his pride. "Get out, you sniveling sycophant!"

Boram hunched through the doorway without a riposte.

When he was gone, Wilam said, "Be careful of that one. He has a mean streak in him that is worse than his father's; and he has the will to carry out what Charel only intimates."

"I have long been aware of that." Sheena tended to her father's needs and helped him to his private chamber. She made him comfortable at his computer console. "It is not good for you to let him upset you. You must remain impassive. Treat him as you would treat a stubborn mathematical equation or a difficult scientific problem. He is nothing more than an obstacle in the path of truth."

"But a very serious obstacle, and one that riles me with his arrogance. In many ways I fear him more than I fear his father, for while they both have ambition, Boram cares little for acceptance by the Council: his method is reactionary, whereas Charel is largely bluff."

Sheena bristled. "If we are not careful, they will both lead us to death, each in his own way."

"That is why we must convince the Council of the gravity of our plight before they let the world ride into oblivion. Tomas, our chief engineer, has rigged some devices for measuring the swings in the magnetic flux that generates our electricity, and reports that our situation is perilous — as if an uncontrolled magnetic storm churns beneath us with growing fury. Already one-third of the collectors have been destroyed by acutely high amplitudes. Tomas has invented a governor that is undergoing trial installation; if it works, it may prevent further loss of resources — at least temporarily."

Wilam plugged himself into the computer probes.

"Father, you must rest. Your work is draining you — "

"I can rest later. Now I must study, I must learn. There is an untapped potential within Erbridge's computer — knowledge that was input so long ago that no one remembers how to extract it. If I lose power, the secrets of the world will go unraveled, perhaps forever. I cannot — I cannot even take time to enjoy my own daughter . . . "

"Father — "

"I am sorry, Sheena. Please try to understand. You know I love you. I loved your mother, too—very much. And she loved us both. But that longing between us did not prevent our planned course of action. We made a pact that our happiness was subordinate to the greater cause. When your mother left the castle, she did not abandon us. She went on a mission as you have done,

Entropy

to solve the puzzle of our existence before we were destroyed by ignorance. And she fully expected to rejoin us. To my great sorrow, Katha has not returned. But you and I must carry on her mission or it will all have been for naught."

"Father, I acknowledge all that. I have never felt abandoned. I want only for you to slow down before you collapse. Take care of your — "

"Sheena, my baby, thank you for your concern and ministrations, but you do not fully comprehend the pressure I am under. Your body is young and responsive, a delight both to have and behold; mine is old and decaying. You have strength to hold yourself together, while I grow weak and flabby. This body is an encumbrance, a prison, a torture chamber, whose feebleness and ailments prevent full concentration on my work. In youth, my body gave me great pleasure, especially when melded with your mother's; but now I live only for the mind and what I hope to accomplish with it."

Sheena anguished over her father's suffering and increasing invalidism. She shuddered to think how awful it must be to lose one's vigor, to feel one's flesh wasting away through age and disease. "Your work can wait for a while — "

"No, it most decidedly cannot. We both have much to do and great distances to travel — I in my mind through electronic circuits, you in your body in the vast frontier."

"Even wanderlust wears thin from fatigue. I have only just returned — "

"And as much as it grieves me, my baby, you must leave immediately on another errand of enlightenment — a journey possibly longer than the last, with results perhaps every bit as strange."

Sheena started to protest but Wilam rushed on.

"I have developed some bizarre theories about our place in the world — and how this world came to be as it is. The evidence you brought back confirms some of my suspicions, but it also opens a whole new parcel of doubts. When I subjoin my scientific discoveries, I get even more confusion. Do you remember the gravitometer you helped me place in the lower level?"

Sheena yielded to his mental digressions. "Yes."

Wilam seemed pleased. "Since then I have established an array of gravitometer stations at various depths and heights. In your absence I have had the help of a young lad in their placement. He even designed a recording graph. As expected, there are minute differences in gravitation relevant to height. But what I also found were irregular deviations in the force of gravity that correspond to two other phenomena: quakes and magnetism."

Suddenly, Sheena's interest was piqued.

"The graphs revealed that a surge in the force of gravity occurred simultaneously with each quake, and that the severity of the quake was directly proportional to the intensity of the surge. Furthermore, a dramatic increase in magnetic flux accompanied the quakes with precise correlation in both magnitude and duration."

Sheena pondered the implications. "A direct cause and effect. Gravity and magnetism are somehow interrelated."

"And their interaction generates quakes. But I need more data before I can determine where these forces originate and, hopefully, understand why they are growing in severity." Wilam painfully made his way to a shelf on which rested a complicated scientific instrument. "When you left before, I was reluctant to let you go; now I implore you to get away before Charel convinces the Council that your existence is a threat to their authority. I have here a compact gravitometer and an automatic recording graph that I want you to carry to the far parts of the world, in the direction I have specified in the instructions. It is important that you adhere closely — "

"But, Father, what if — " Sheena faltered while she gathered her thoughts, and put her feelings in perspective. "What if I am gone so long that — you are not here — to utilize . . . "

"Sheena, my baby." Wilam gathered his daughter

close to him. They clung together for a long moment of tenderness. "You remind me so much of your mother. And although she has been gone from my presence, she has never been gone from my mind. We are always together in spirit."

Sheena separated from her father's embrace. "That is not the same."

"Of course not. But neither can we be together if the world splits us apart. We must do what we can to preserve this world; our work transcends all else. And we can only hope that when we pass from this plane of existence there is a better one awaiting us."

Chapter 11

"Ahoy, there."

Marek practically jumped out of his skin. He drew his sword in an instant and held it at the ready.

"Greetings." Sheena kept her weapon sheathed. To Marek, "He is a stranger, a savage. There is no need for swordplay."

The man who advanced openly through the brush was old and disheveled, with a midriff that sagged ungracefully. His armor was dirty, his robe tattered. On his back he carried a stringed device and a pouch full of leafed staffs.

"Wanderers be rare in these parts, what with the sweepers and all thick as flocks. Got to keep on the alert, you do, else you get beamed, drilled, or pecked to death for your woes. Name be Freder. What be yours and where be you going?"

The knoll was open and craggy, and stood so high above the effervescent swamp that vegetation did not thrive. Exposed rocks were encrusted with cusps of dried foliage. A thin mist hovered in the air.

"Sheena. My companion is Marek."

As unobtrusively as possible, Marek slipped his blade into its sheath. "Greetings, stranger."

Sheena was noncommittal. "We are on an exploratory trek."

"We be all, at that."

"We come from Erbridge," Marek added in a friendly manner.

"Erbridge? Erbridge? What means that? We be all from Erbridge."

Marek got no help from Sheena. "It is the name of our castle."

"A castle named after the world? How unoriginal."

"Excuse my companion's lack of sophistication. He is young and this is his first trek. Travel is not encouraged by our elders."

"No blame for that. Erbridge be a hostile place where only the shrewd survive. Which brings me to me point. Got some sweepers coming this way you might want to avoid. Big ones with big guns."

Sheena knew exactly what he meant. "Thank you, Freder, for the intelligence. Marek, we must be going."

"Why? What are sweepers?"

Freder was dumbfounded. "You spend your life in a dungeon?"

Again Sheena let Marek fend for himself. "I — I — that is, in the castle we did not have . . . "

"Boy got a lot to learn." Freder turned his attention to Sheena. "But teach him later." He indicated the small creatures scuttling across the ground on double rows of stalks tipped with sharp talons; they did not slow their flight to use them. "Critters be on the move. So, which way go you?"

"For now, away from the sweepers. Would you care to join us?"

"Thanks for the hospitality. I would. Got no commitments except not to get mistook for vermin."

A large animal poked its long proboscis into the clearing. It stood on four jointed members that locked rigidly to hold the body upright; its tail was barbed and dripped venom. As it hunched back and prepared to spring, Freder whirled into action. He unslung his stringed device, notched a leafed staff, aimed, and let fly. The steel-tipped staff embedded itself deep into the animal's hide; it collapsed instantly.

"I suggest we move before the sweepers drive out more of them." Freder kept his weapon ready. "Or something worse."

Sheena was already on the move. "Good advice."

They angled away from the swamp, down the side of the hill that was less steep and easier to climb, and which led into a forest that was only sparsely covered with underbrush. The tops of the trees were lost in fog; the middles hosted a wide variety of clawed animals that clung to the bark or danced across drooping vines. Airborne critters hovered in thick clouds.

"What are sweepers?" Marek wanted to know.

"What we call demons."

"Demons? Demons?" Freder could hardly control his mirth. "That be rich. You people must come from the real outback. And them blades you carry be useless. You can strike only from touching distance, and by that time you be dead."

"Swords are used against swords," Marek explained. "In person-to-person combat."

Freder suddenly became serious. "What mean you by that? Why would a person fight his friend?"

Once more Marek was on the spot without Sheena to back him. "Because — because — to control the masses, or to fend off attack, or — "

Sheena found herself unfairly enjoying Marek's embarrassment. His description of life within the castle walls, of the subjugation of the people, of a bloodthirsty Council, all painted a picture that was beyond the simple imagination of the wayward savage. She finally came to the young guard's rescue.

"You can understand why we left home. Life under those conditions was intolerable. And you are right — we live so far in the outback that our people have had no communication with the rest of the world in more generations than anyone remembers. Emissaries neither come nor go. Brotherhood is a lost concept."

"If that be the case, I have reached midpoint in me trek and return to the sea. Sweepers I can manage, but fighting people be not to me liking. It be unnatural. And, if it be true, being killed by me own kind excites me even less."

The flight of fear-struck herds was becoming more evident. Small furry beasts passed quickly along the ground without paying attention to the people in their way. Swarms of airborne creatures flapped by with sharpened beaks extended. Most of the animals, however, were harmless.

"They be too scared to stick us."

Nonetheless, Marek ducked the flocks and their pointed extremities. "Do the demons — the sweepers —

Entropy

do this often?"

"Always. Got to rid the world of vermin. But they beam a person as quick as anything else. Some believe it be a flaw in their programming."

"Perhaps people were never intended to roam the forests," Sheena offered.

"Not much choice with the tunnels full of mutated flesh." Freder studied the terrain as they kept pace with the migrating hordes. They passed through a thicket, then entered a circular clearing surrounded by tall trees. He searched the ground until he found a patch of grass growing by itself. He flipped over the patch to reveal an electrical socket. He jammed dirt into the contact holes. "That will slow them down a bit."

Sheena was impressed. "A cute trick."

"By the time they dig it out, we be gone. Works all the time." Freder smoothed the grass patch back over the charging port. "Got to outwit them at their own game. We get out of their sweep path, and we be okay." Freder led them on a course diagonal to that of the stampeding hordes and down into the marshes. "The sweepers hate the swamps. Shorts out their electrical circuits."

Soon they left the animal masses behind. The marsh gas hung thick over putrid puddles. Slimy apods slinking along the bottomlands did not seem to mind the intrusion; others floated idly on broad green leaves that bobbed gently on the ripples.

"So you folks grew up in the security of a castle? No envy. Not after those tales."

"It is worse than that. Our leaders are so afraid of being overthrown by truth that they have sent the palace guards to slay us. With such danger following, you might consider leaving us to our lot."

"And leave a pretty lass like you to fate? That be not me manner. I think I tag along."

"We are glad to have you."

Marek could not contain his curiosity any longer. "Freder, what is that strange device that propels sticks so straight and far?"

Freder unlimbered his weapon and showed it to him. "A crossbow. Are they unknown in your part of the world?" Marek fondled the wooden stock while Freder showed him how to crank back the string. "The arrow lies in this groove, be notched against the string, and released by the trigger. The leaves on the end stabilize its flight. Deadly accurate it be, and the steel tip will penetrate most sweeper's hulls."

"Might I try it later?"

"I will give you lessons. But it be for defense only — not against people."

"Even people who attack?" Sheena argued.

Freder ruminated over the contradiction. "A new experience, that. The world be constantly changing, and not for the good. But when people fight each other, the time of judgment be not far off, and the Great Collapse shall follow."

"Then you should know that the purpose of our journey is to stay the Great Collapse."

Freder was so stunned that he stopped in his tracks. "In that case, there be more danger before you than behind." Lost in thought, he slung the crossbow over his back and slipped it into its carrier. The arrow went back into the quiver. "What makes you think mere mortals can do what the Ancients could not?"

"My father was a great scientist. He studied physics and natural history, and examined lost data in the computer network. He discovered vast forces at work — forces external to the world but which influence its movements. It was his belief that the Great Collapse predicted by legend has a basis in fact, that it is controlled by an energy source of a size beyond our comprehension, that we are caught in its grip, and that the Sacred Portal is a passageway into a new eternity."

"Deep thoughts, but meaningless to me. I be a common boater."

Marek lent support. "Neither do I understand the significance of the legends. Wilam taught me many facts, but only he had the capacity to interpret them."

"Perhaps. But I be smart enough to know the world

Entropy

be on the brink of disaster. Great whirlpools make ocean commerce impossible. Many a boat and many a good rower be dragged down into the depths of the sea. That be why I left me occupation to roam the hostile land. Sweepers can be avoided once you learn their tricks and routes, but not a vortex that appears suddenly without warning."

Sheena's interest was piqued. "Do you refer to the sparkling sea across the magic mountains?"

"That be the one — the only one. Spent me life rowing trade goods between the coastal castles. I be strong in me youth, like young Marek here, and the work be hard and rewarding. Time changes. What with commlink breakdowns, we boaters became messengers, carrying dispatches to keep the people informed on worldwide events. The tidings be never good. Great waves wash against the shore taking away wharfs and piles, people and underpinnings. Strange currents tear out the beaches. Boats and their crews disappear. People be scared of what be next."

"What are they doing about it?"

"They be praying. None have I met but you with the temerity to challenge the forces of nature."

"You disapprove?"

"Not me place to interfere with the fancies of others."

"Well put, but do you disapprove?"

"Mere mortals cannot change the course of the world. I think you suffer from delusions to the contrary."

"Your tact is unbounded." Sheena persisted with growing impatience. "So answer me this — will you aid us in our quest?"

Freder delayed his response so long that the three of them assumed the frozen poise of a tableau. He appeared to be in dilemma. "You interest me, Lass; and your young friend, too. But what can a humble boater do to help you in your quest?"

"Since you have already crossed the magic mountains you must know the route."

"That be true."

"And since you are a boater you must know the sea."

"Truer still. I have crossed only once the magic mountains, but have rowed many times round the world."

"And how many times have you crossed the sparkling sea?"

Again Freder was disturbed by an uncomfortable question. He made several faltering starts before admitting his fears. "There be old superstitions about the other side of the sea — that the distance across be infinity, that the far shore be the beachhead of immortality, that beyond lies the gateway to the Sacred Portal and a land of great expanse."

"Are you a superstitious person?"

"I be a pragmatist, or try to be."

"Do you believe the superstitions about the sparkling sea?"

"As much as any superstition."

Sheena was frustrated as diplomacy degenerated to evasion. Although Freder was too honest to lie, he was also too smart to box himself in as a skeptic. She tried a different tack. "Are you an adventurous person?"

"That be the reason I climbed the magic mountains — to find out for meself what the world be like in the untamed inland."

"Why, then, did you never venture to row across the sea? You are a boater, with a boater's skills."

"Curiosity be me guide, but fear be me restraint. Here, at least, the dangers be known, and weapons exist to fight them. Besides, nowhere be there a crew daft enough to try it."

"Then perhaps our ways should part."

"Perhaps. But I like your spunk and quest for adventure, even though you be crazy. Will take you over the magic mountains and point you to the coast. Got the spirit for that. But when it comes to crossing the sea, you be on your own. May the Ancients be with you."

Chapter 12
Flashback

The castle rampart was oddly familiar, giving Sheena a strange feeling of déjà vu. It was a near duplicate of Erbridge but without the sentries. The parapet was intact, the moat filled, the drawbridge partially lowered. A sign on the ramp offered instructions.

Sheena flipped open the protective cap and pressed the button inside the liquid-tight housing. Massive motors came into play. The drawbridge cranked down on gears that could have used a little grease. It halted twice along the way. When the platform reached ground level, it was misaligned with the apron and the edge overhung.

Cautiously, Sheena jumped up onto the drawbridge and waited patiently for something to happen. The invitation was obvious, but not within her experience. She was about to skulk into the castle when an old crone emerged suddenly from the guardhouse embedded in the wall.

"Welcome, Milady. Welcome. Sorry no one was here to greet you officially, but we get so few visitors anymore that the gate goes untended. I just happened to be passing by on an errand. Have you been waiting long?"

Sheena did not know quite how to respond to such a friendly overture. The crone was unarmed, and wore a dress that was clean and neat without being gaudy. Her posture was stooped with age, yet her bearing was maintained by strong inner poise. She exuded genuine cordiality.

"Actually, I just got here."

"So come on in. Come on in."

Sheena shuffled forward with more than a little timidity. "I am surprised that access to your castle is encouraged."

"Why should it be otherwise? The drawbridge is designed to keep out sweepers, not people. The mechanical monsters create havoc when they slip in unannounced." In aside, "Got to keep the little buggers in phase, you know."

"You mean, they are allowed within the ramparts?"

"Of course. Of course. How else to electrocute the vermin and prevent them from overtaking the castle? We calibrate their programming before they come in, you know. Their memory chips have a nasty habit of transmitting crossed signals — something to do with false magnetic imprinting from acute fluxion. Not being a scientist, my understanding of the mechanism is meager. But even an old crackbrain like me can tell the problem is getting worse. So where you from?"

"Erbridge."

"Did not think you were from the stars. What is the name of your castle?"

"We call it Erbridge."

"A bit egocentric, but permissible. So, welcome to Grange. I am Lilla."

"Sheena."

"Pleased to meet you, Sheena. Pleased to meet you." They stopped outside the guardhouse. Lilla turned her attention to a control board and pressed a sequence of buttons. Thick chains drew the bridge to an upright position. "Got to get the bearings realigned. That last quake threw the foundations a bit out of kilter."

"I felt it a ways back. It shook down trees and knocked me to the ground. I could not move until it stopped."

"They come more often, too, than when I was a girl." In aside, "Of course, that was when the world was still young." Lilla slammed the guardhouse door. "No sense taking you through the transducts, you being a guest." The portcullis rose on well-oiled slides. It jammed halfway up, and Lilla had to bump it free; then it continued smoothly. "Remind me to make a work note on that. If the Committee gets too slack, they will find themselves ousted at the next election."

Once inside, Lilla pressed another button that reversed the motors of the portcullis; the armored gate

Entropy

lowered into place. "So what brings you to our part of the woods?"

The old woman was so ingenuous that Sheena found herself explaining secrets withheld from the Council under penalty of death. "Partly exploration, partly to take systematic measurements of natural phenomena."

Lilla led Sheena to a motor cart and invited her to board. "Any goods to trade?"

"No. I have nothing but the scientific instruments necessary for my work."

"Too bad. Sad to say, we do not get the number of visitors we used to. Miss the company as much as the commerce. We still get shipments from the close neighbors, those still producing, but our contacts are declining. Some of the castles are going out of business, and the people are moving out."

"To become wanderers, like the savages?"

"Some, but mostly they move into a better equipped castle." The cart hummed along a road only slightly humped by ground displacement. Fog clung to the vine-covered trees that lined the road. "Population is down all over. With the very ground breaking up beneath us, some folks are afraid to start families. Waiting for better times. Got a long wait, I think."

The crone's dress flapped in the breeze as the cart picked up speed on the straightaway. Pedestrians ambled along the sidewalks seemingly without a care. Several waved, and Lilla waved back. Gardens resplendent with blossoming flowers dotted neatly trimmed lawns, adding color to an already colorful environment.

"Where are you taking me?"

"A hospitality suite, so you can freshen up. Got lots of rooms due to the paucity of visitors. Have your pick of accommodations. Rules are that if you decide to stay a while, you got to move into lower level quarters and contribute some of your time to the public good. Other than that, you are on your own."

"That is very kind," Sheena acknowledged. The differences between the operation of Grange and Erbridge were so vast that she thought it advisable to keep them to herself, lest she get caught in long explanations.

"Just routine."

The central spire appeared much like the Citadel of Erbridge, except that no sentries guarded the gates to the inner courtyard. Lilla parked the cart, plugged in the charging cord, and led the way inside. Children splashed in the fountain and gamboled about unattended; closely cropped grass offered a resilient playing surface.

Sheena was uplifted by the joyous frolic. "They seem so cheerful."

"Ah, to be young again, and not appreciate the true state of the world. Maturity brings with it such awful responsibility."

The interior of the spire was plain and uncluttered, with none of the gold and jeweled trappings that gave the Citadel its garish opulence. The fixtures were pretty but functional and simplistic. People meandered through open cubicles that exhibited everything from tools to toys to works of art. The upper levels branching off the ramp held airy rooms full of murals, statues, and dioramas. The spire was largely a museum.

"The upper floor for you, Milady." Lilla escorted her to a private room with its own bath facilities. "Make yourself at home while I fetch Daker. He will want to debrief you."

Then Sheena was alone. She set her pack on a countertop and removed the instruments in order to take readings and enter them in her log. Once her work was done, she began to relax. As she shed her clothing, she felt the weight of her adventures slip away. She had been a long time on the trail, a long time fighting rogue sweepers and deadly beasts. Once she got caught in the beam path between a sweeper and the drove of many-limbed creatures it was trying to cull; her armor was singed, but she escaped unscathed.

Now it all seemed so distant, as if the world outside the castle rampart was in another dimension. Here there was security, even if only temporary — until the

Entropy

next big quake or pressure wave. Sheena bathed long and languorously. Afterward, she donned a deep-pile guest robe. She took her time washing her clothes and, after recouping her vigor, she polished her armor. For the moment she quit being an aggressive warrior and became a plain female. It was a luxury she had seldom allowed herself.

Later, a male announced himself on the intercom.

Sheena opened the door for him. "Please come in. I am Sheena."

"Yes, Lilla told me about you. I am Daker, a duly elected member of the Committee. One of my responsibilities is meeting visitors in order to discuss world affairs. We are concerned about the increasing incidence and severity of natural catastrophes, and wonder how others are being affected by them."

"That is exactly why I have embarked upon this journey. My father is chief scientist of our castle. He has sent me to study the nature of the world with the hope of discovering the underlying causes of its instability." Sheena showed Daker her notes and instruments. "There appear to be underground stress factors wherever I go."

Daker's concern was obvious. "That is very interesting. No one to my knowledge has ever undertaken field tests such as yours. We used to communicate frequently with neighboring castles until the commlinks broke down between us. With increasing isolation over recent generations, news of outside events shrank while ignorance and apathy increased.

"Each time the ground moved, our tunnel transportation network became more inoperable. The compartments shifted out of alignment, the bulkheads bent, the hatches would not seal, and some of the tunnels flooded while others were evacuated — as if cracks or rifts opened into great caverns far beneath the surface.

"I am told that we used to trade freely with castles the world over. Now we live in virtual insularity. Most people are afraid of surface travel because of wild beasts and maladjusted sweepers that fail to recognize security signals. We keep a few trade routes open by posting armed patrols, but even those are on the wane. We are turning into ourselves, becoming more introverted, internalizing our anxieties without reaching out for solutions . . . "

Sheena sensed Daker's frustration. "There is no need to make excuses. The fault is not yours."

"But I feel so helpless. We all do. We seem to have — lost courage. The Ancients had some purpose, some grand design in constructing all this." Daker indicated the immediate environs. "It is as if we are being punished for not keeping the faith, for not carrying out their magnificent scheme. They built these castles and interconnecting tunnels for a reason that has been lost with the passage of time. And we who have inherited the product of their technology have strayed from the path of truth."

"You bear more of a burden than is yours to bear."

"Perhaps." Daker was not mollified. "And perhaps because we have forsaken the meaning of it all we must now pay the price."

"A fatalistic attitude." Sheena pointed to the instruments spread out on the counter. "The data gathered during my journey is already falling into a pattern. I am certain that continued corroboration will help unravel the mystery of this world of ours — and hopefully lead to a viable solution."

Daker picked up one of the devices. "What do these do?"

"That is a coriolimeter. It reads deflection of the coriolis force. One of my father's greatest discoveries is that Erbridge is a rotating body suspended in empty space. Motion is translated into a vector that this instrument calculates. Of course, the strength of the force is subject to local variation due to altitude — "

Daker waved her off. "You are getting way beyond me."

"Sorry." Sheena pointed to the needle on the top. "In simple terms, it is a direction finder. Since leaving my

Entropy

castle, I have kept a constant bearing except where my path was blocked by broad chasms. Because the surface of Erbridge is curved, as long as I do not deviate from my course, I should eventually return to my place of origin."

"Indeed?" Daker was noticeably upset by Sheena's revelations.

Sheena touched the brass casing of another device. "This is a radiometer; it detects the spontaneous emission of particles from unstable elements. This one is an electrometer to detect atomic wave patterns. I have found that both forms of radiation increase with depth; that is, the deeper tunnels are more radioactive than the shallower tunnels. And I have found intense bursts of radiation accompanying seismic activity. Furthermore, I have approached chasms opened after disruptive quakes. On several occasions when great quantities of air were being sucked down into a seemingly bottomless abyss, I found strong radiation that faded in direct proportion to the diminishing airflow. When the suction ceased, radiation returned to its normal background level."

"You describe phenomena that are beyond my comprehension." Daker shunned the rest of Sheena's instruments. "I am not a scientist. I do not understand these things. But I do appreciate the importance of knowledge. Sheena, will you accompany me upramp to visit Prissa?"

Sheena shrugged. "If you wish."

"Prissa is our chief scientist, a woman of brilliance. Her mind grasps concepts that the rest of us find — unintelligible. Some think she is insane. For a long time she has been doing computer simulations on mathematical models of something she calls the Universe. Perhaps an exchange of information will give each of you a better appreciation of the history of the world, and the forces that are reducing it to dust."

Prissa's cubicle stood at the extreme pinnacle of the spire, and was little more than a computer terminal with ancillary input connections. The chief scientist squatted in a circular tub; she was a nearly shapeless mass of such extreme age that it was a wonder to Sheena that her body still pulsed with life. A doctor was in attendance, monitoring the flow of liquids through plastic tubes into her ghastly, misshapen torso.

"Her body no longer functions as it should; she has difficulty assimilating nutriments on her own," Daker explained. "Only constant attention and medical science has kept her alive. She survives in limbo. It seems ages since she last returned to her physical being. Although her torment is excruciating, we hope she will not die."

Sheena was reminded of the constant agony suffered by her father. "Has she no choice in the matter?"

"This is her free will."

Sheena could not help but feel anguish for what Prissa was enduring in order to maintain her mental activity. The scientist must have more than a great mind — she must have noble resolve to yield her body to a state of perpetual paralysis so her mind could be free to interact with the computer.

Sheena noticed the spare set of input leads. "May I get into the computer?"

"You must. It is the only way to communicate with her."

She squeezed into the console, attached the suction cups of the input leads, and plugged the wires into the terminal sockets. The access codes were identical to those employed by Erbridge's central processing unit. As she made the mental connections with the data bank, she opened her synapses to the electronic circuits of the computer. Her thoughts flowed from the organic braincase of their origin into the mainframe receptors, melding one to the other, permitting Sheena to roam freely through the computer's circuitry while still maintaining conscious awareness of her physical surroundings. She could hold conversations both chemically and mechanically.

"Is she awake?" Daker asked.

"I have not yet found her." Sheena searched

Entropy

through the programs for the one of which Prissa was a part. The scientist was deeply integrated and difficult to extract from the main database; she had been in there so long without remission that the strength of her personality had faded. "She is coming up now, but she is very weak."

"Who calls me?"

"My name is Sheena."

"Leave me alone. I am computing."

"Thinking, Prissa. You are thinking."

"I do not distinguish the two."

"You are not a program, Prissa. You are a person, a being of flesh and blood."

"Who are you to tell me what I am?"

"I am a scientist, an explorer. I am conducting field tests on the forces that influence the world, and have data in which you might be interested."

"Then enter your data and leave the processing to me."

Sheena picked up her logbook and read the entries. "I want something in return."

"I do not have to give you anything."

Sheena applied reverse feedback. "Why else are programs written?"

Prissa was momentarily looped in a logic circuit. Sheena knew computer programming well enough to break all but the most convoluted coding systems. The person/circuit that identified herself/itself as Prissa fought the flaw in her software.

"I do not require much of your time, Prissa."

"Time? Time? What is time to me? Time can be compressed until it no longer passes, and it can stretch forever. Space can be contracted to the point of nothingness, and it can expand to infinity. But neither can exist without the other; they are inseparable. Space-time is everything, both instantaneous and eternal."

Sheena wondered if these ramblings were due to derangement, senility, or long-term computer linking. Can a flow of electrons have hallucinations? "I want to know about the Universe."

"You do not ask much, only for a lifetime of research condensed to a definition."

Her response was a good sign: computers could not be sarcastic. "An outline will do for the present. The details you can imprint on a crystal transfile."

"You expect me to give you all the results of my studies?"

"The purpose of computation is to generate data for the user. For every input there must be output."

Sheena hit the right combination. The code was broken. But she felt that the outpouring of information was transferred with great reluctance. She inserted a transmission file that she could take back to her father. As the data were digitized within the lattice, she skimmed topic titles and abstracts that read like ramblings of the insane.

"The Universe exists in delicate balance. Like a pendulum, it swings between creation and destruction, beginning and end, life and death. The Universe that always was, always will be. Now it is neither . . .

"The same forces that create the Universe will destroy it. And the same forces that destroy the Universe will create it. That is inevitable . . .

"The Universe consists of one barrier after another: barriers of space and barriers of time. And, like the rampart that surrounds the castle, like the wall around the world, there is always another side . . .

"Erbridge is not alone in the Universe. There are billions and billions of worlds stretched throughout the vastness of space like grains of sand on a beach, like motes of dust in the air, like atoms in the brain. But Erbridge is the only one with a purpose . . . "

But what purpose?

"The balance of the Universe is about to be tipped, but I do not know in which direction. That is the final allegory, the great elusive truth that we both seek. Help me find the way."

"I cannot," Sheena told her. "I am lost myself."

Chapter 13

"Did you really do it?" Marek was last in line as the trio forged through a low-lying area that was neither swamp nor veldt, but a damp cross between the two. "Did you return to Erbridge from the opposite direction?"

"Yes." Sheena ambled along with seeming unconcern. "Although I admit that when I started out I had my doubts about Father's theories."

"Any fool knows the world be round. How else could it be?"

"Freder, you forget that we grew up in a castle where the people were purposely kept in ignorance. The control of knowledge was the Council's way of exalting themselves and preserving their influence. That was why my father and I were such a threat to them: because we proved that the Council had no power over nature, only self-ordained dominion over the castle. The people knew only what they were told, without the opportunity to learn on their own. And since we in castle Erbridge did not come from a family of boaters, the outer rampart was our farthest frontier."

"But it just makes sense."

"To you, Freder. But does it make sense that Erbridge is only one of many worlds spinning through space?"

"That be ridiculous."

"No, it is simply beyond your experience. You must concede that there are many things you do not understand. Why are we here? Where did we come from? Where are we going?"

"Those be problems for philosophers. I question how Erbridge can float in this so-called Universe with nothing to hold it up."

"I do not know," Sheena admitted. "But I was in the computer with Prissa. I sampled her data. Her mathematics were sound, her equations were based on well-founded principles of physics. Father could have . . . " Sheena wretched with melancholy, and only with great difficulty fought it off. Why did she vacillate so, one moment longing for his presence, the next making believe his death did not matter? "Given enough time he could have combined her studies with his and formed a cohesive whole."

"This concept of Universe is beyond my comprehension," Marek allowed. "But it is not necessary for me — or for any of us — to understand its workings. Wilam told me that the Sacred Portal is the place of ultimate understanding, that when we find it, all would be made clear."

"What makes you think there *be* a Sacred Portal?"

"The legends — "

"Forget legends. Ignore myths. Cancel your beliefs. There be nothing real that cannot be touched."

Sheena warily skirted an animal hole. "Can one touch gravity, or magnetism?"

"That be different." Freder led the way up a gradual slope shrouded in perpetual mist. For a long time they had been traveling fast, without the impediments of dense jungle or sinking bogs. "They be forces."

"Then perhaps the Sacred Portal is a force."

Freder ruminated at length over Sheena's pronouncement. Travel became easier as the elevation increased. The ground was only sparsely covered with grass and miniature shrubs. A herd of four-legged beasts stampeded out of the way as if the approaching people were demons on the sweep. Zephyrs scooped up dust and redeposited it capriciously; the land seemed to creep under the constant drift of sand.

"That be a good point."

"Keep an open mind, Freder." Sheena felt at ease on the uphill climb. "When venturing into the unknown one must expect the unanticipated."

"In that you be right." Freder scrambled over a rounded rock that was only the first of a field of boulders. The sandstone surfaces were weathered by the prevailing wind, and in many places pitted deeply.

Entropy

Beyond lay a valley whose extent was lost in the mist.
"Ahoy, there!"

Sheena cringed instinctively. "Palace guards."

The uniform was unmistakable. They were strung in a cordon below a low escarpment a short distance in front. Strong gusts of air whipped the dust around them, but not thick enough to disguise the row of raised swords.

Marek mounted the rock beside Sheena. "Worse than that. It is Charel himself."

"I give you greetings, Sheena, Marek, and stranger. I have come a long way to discuss issues of great importance. We mean you no harm."

Freder backed until he was flanked by his companions. "Be these the evil men you told me about?"

Sheena drew her sword with calm deliberation. "They are."

"Forgive me for doubting you." Freder shrank behind them and checked their path of retreat. "Action belies his rhetoric. I like it not when people show blades to proclaim peaceful intent."

The guards were a bedraggled lot: their clothing was torn, their filigree gone, their armor singed. Missing scales exposed raw wounds that armor no longer protected. Once strong, and the choice of the corps, their spirit seemed to have sagged.

Charel came forward behind the protection of five guards arranged in a semicircle and forming a phalanx. "My son made a mistake that I do not mean to repeat."

"Then do not underestimate me as he did. It could be fatal." Sheena advanced to meet Charel's challenge. "Repetition is in *my* control, not yours."

"I do not want to fight you, Sheena."

She advancing steadily, sword outstretched. "To cross me is to fight me. To fight me is to die."

"I forgive you for killing Boram."

"I did not kill the conniver. I released him as he released my father. Both were in great pain."

Charel's guards approached at an ever-slowing pace. Charel drew his sword and used it as a prod.

"Quit the platitudes, Sheena, and let us get down to business. Your father's death was an unfortunate accident; Boram acted out of turn. But it is done. I have half an army below me prepared to charge at my command. They can smother you easily by sheer weight of numbers. But enough lives have already been exchanged. If you lay down your weapons and return to Erbridge now, I promise you a place of prominence. You will be the first female Council member."

"An attractive proposition that once would have swayed my allegiance."

"My offer is sincere."

Marek rushed to Sheena's side and placed his blade by hers. "Do not believe him. He wants only to use you to regain the confidence of the people."

"Marek, my once and faithful servant. Why have you turned against me?"

"I was never your servant, and never faithful. Those are your delusions."

Charel maintained a facade of utter calm. "Remember that when you turn against me, vengeance is mine to mete."

The guards halted their advance. Sheena and Marek stopped a blade's length away. Charel huddled behind the wall of guards as if they formed an impregnable stone rampart. Tension bristled in the air as palpable as electric discharge.

"I want you alive, Sheena, if you will come willingly. But diplomacy has its limits, and my patience wears thin."

"True to form, if you cannot get what you want by pledge, you try to take it by force."

Charel ignored her recriminations. "You can help quell the civil war by explaining to the people that only by working together can we hope to master the cataclysmic events that overtake us. Bring your evidence before the Council, let us review your data." He gesticulated wildly. "Surely your father told you that there were those among us who acknowledged the relevance of his work — "

Entropy

Sheena did know, but she had no idea that Charel was one of them. Her mind raced with revelation, and her resolve momentarily swayed.

" — who understood its implications. Yes, we admit that evil energy stirs the world from beneath the seemingly solid surface." Charel motioned histrionically; his sword weaved in emphasis. "Wilam was close to discovering the solution to these ills when he met his untimely end. But his mind betrayed him. He was tortured so by physical pain that his thought processes were affected — "

She knew it was true. In the brief time they had together, when she locked in the transmission file so he could access Grange's data, she felt the torment of his body. Her mind wandered back to those final tragic moments when Wilam was plugged into his computer console with only the sheer force of will to keep him alive; as long as he was free to think he could suffer his body's agonizing convulsions.

" — He was not able to concentrate. He was distracted, distraught, barely in control of his body. A lesser person would have given in — "

Charel twirled his sword like a baton, swung his dagger in consort. Sheena snapped back to attention when she recognized her enemy's oratory diversion. The dagger was upheld and poised for flight but had not yet left his grip when a steel-tipped arrow thwacked through the air and pinned the carved hilt to flesh. Charel writhed in pain.

Without an instant's hesitation, Freder spun the crossbow's crank and notched another arrow. "He be going to kill you." Another arrow cleaved the space between two guards and transfixed Charel's sword. The Council member was crucified upon his own weapons.

Sheena and Marek lunged simultaneously, and two palace guards fell flat. The other three wasted no time falling back from suddenly uneven odds. Charel was forced to stumble downhill to avoid being tromped by his own contingent.

"Our route be across yonder valley so well guarded

by swords." Freder yanked another arrow from his quiver. "But I not be liking this campaign against people."

"We will try to outflank them, but keep your crossbow loaded. They have the advantage of position. Marek, take the lead."

Charel's army was on the move even as the Council member retreated. He dropped to the ground in torment, but not so incapacitated that he could not order his troops into battle. The palace guards clambered slowly up ledges they could easily have bounded.

"They charge warily, if such a maneuver be possible."

Marek raced along the upper lip of the valley, leaping from boulder to boulder with agility out of context with his size. Small creatures skittered out of the way and melted into crevices like flaccid jelly. Marek paid them no notice. Not until he reached a gully did he stop to let the others catch him. "If we drop down here we can get below them."

Sheena trusted his judgment. "Do it."

The hard downhill climb took them past Charel's troops before the enemy knew they had been outsmarted. The gully cut deep at first, then leveled out and broke into a short canyon lined with brush and short trees that grew along the edge of a dry streambed. The fog hung high like a cloud. Vast herds of shaggy quadrupeds milled on the valley floor like a carpet.

"The animals be safe from sweepers because their treads be unsuited for climbing cliffs."

"How do we get through?" Marek still held his sword on guard. "Do we slash our way across?"

"They be high-strung but harmless." Freder waded into the nearest concentration of furred flesh as a way of demonstrating his point. The beasts were twice his height, with rounded bodies that were soft and smooth and seemingly omnidirectional: they bounced off each other like a box full of balloons. Soon Freder was lost among them. "Stay close lest we be separated. The base of the magic mountains lies on the other side of the valley."

Marek faltered before the solid wall of flesh that towered above him. "I do not relish being crushed."

"They be mostly air sacs that deflate easily."

Sheena grabbed Marek and pulled him into the melee of ricocheting animals. "Sheath your sword lest you accidentally stab one of the beasts."

Marek did as he was told. Soon they were all hidden by large numbers of hairy quadrupeds. Sheena felt the long, coarse strands scrape her armor as the animals brushed by in erratic locomotion — as if the herd were a giant living whirligig. Each time she was squeezed between two fat bodies, she felt an initial pressure that was soon released as the air sacs bulged around her, engulfing her, and the animal rebounded like a rubber ball.

"This be kind of fun."

Marek was not so amused. "I have never played with animals before. Those that live in the castle have vile habits and carry disease, and need to be hunted down and killed. They infest the living quarters with their plague."

"Be kind to your sweepers and they be kind to you."

Sheena allowed herself to be bumped around even though she was sometimes shoved aside from the most direct route; it was easier to yield than to fight. "My experience with sweepers is that they all suffer from function faults."

"That be true in my experience as well. But many be correctable."

"Perhaps. But magnetic anomalies have destroyed so much original programming that the rogues outnumber the sweepers that can be rewritten to operate properly. Each flux does more irreversible damage. And generations ago similar magnetic disturbance was responsible for destroying the computer links between castles, fragmenting civilization into sequestered communes."

"Aye. The world be in a terrible state. These peregrinations have taught me more than I wanted to know.

When people kill their fellows for having different beliefs, the end be not far off."

They broke into a clearing where a low butte rose above the herds. Freder hopped up short ledges to the flat top. Sheena and Marek joined him. Not far away the talus sloped upward at a consistent angle until it was swallowed by the ever-present mist.

"That be the beginning of our ascent."

"Then let us hurry on our way." Sheena climbed down from the rise and plowed into the rambling herd. "We will rest more easily on the summit."

Marek was right behind her, forcing his bulk between the stringy locks of animals. "Freder, is it true that one can fly from the top of the magic mountains?"

"No. But you can jump so high that you will never come down."

Chapter 14
Flashback

"Empiricism is the basis of science. An honest scholar accepts the results of his experiments, then interprets those results with respect to other observable phenomena."

Wilam closed his mind to the images flashing through the circuits of the computer, and concentrated instead on cerebrating with his young protégé. Marek sensed all his master's thoughts and feelings as if both he and Wilam were one person. He was aware of external stimuli on a subconscious level, but most incoming sensations were evoked electronically. Education through computer link was accelerated not only because of the immediate accessibility to data, but because it allowed for no miscommunication between teacher and student.

"But these results are abstractions."

"No, my boy, they are extrapolations of scientific method. There is more to the world than we perceive through our senses. That is why we make devices to detect activity that our physical limitations prevent us from observing directly. We exist in a narrow slot between very small nuclear interactions and very large stellar events, both of which are beyond our means of perception but are every bit as real as the floor that prevents us from falling to the ground."

Marek's thoughts were translated into a pattern of electrons that flowed straight into his mentor's mind. "But if gravity is a force generated by matter, why do two tables not draw toward each other? Why, in fact, does everything not crash together into one all-encompassing mass?"

"Good questions, Marek, for which I have only partial answers. My experiments, via the instruments you helped me build, have disclosed certain basic principles in the structure of the world. But although I have accumulated data on some of the parts, I have yet to assemble those parts into a cohesive whole, or to postulate a theory to account for all the effects of the forces at work."

"Like the disparity between mass and weight?"

Wilam pondered to himself for a moment, his thoughts temporarily blocked from Marek until the aged scientist reopened his mind.

"That disparity lies neither in the equations that differentiate mass from weight, nor in the axioms upon which those equations are based, but in experimental miscorrelation. Our instruments have yielded data that defy common sense."

Marek tripped a memory circuit. "Common sense is logic based upon assumptions made over a lifetime of observation."

"Very good, my boy. Very good. In order to be more specific I should substitute 'longtime affirmation' for 'common sense.' We know that weight is what keeps us on the ground and prevents us from floating up into the air. We know that the deeper we climb the heavier we become, and the higher we ascend the lighter we get. That is why we rest easier at elevation, such as the upper floors of the Citadel, and why our strength is sapped so quickly in the lowest sublevels. We have grown up with that corollary. It makes sense.

"Now comes my discovery that all matter, not just the ground beneath us, exerts a specific, quantifiable gravitational field: a force that attracts all other matter. But that force is minute. Two tables do not move toward each other because the attractive force between them is not strong enough to overcome the friction they exert upon the floor."

Marek interposed. "Does that not imply that enormous mass generates the force that holds us to the ground?"

"So it would seem. What we interpret subjectively as weight is a function of gravity upon matter. But the strength of a gravitational field diminishes exponentially with distance."

Entropy

"Then everything falls into place."

Wilam ignored the unintentional quip. "Again, so it would seem. But when I calculate the force of gravity necessary to hold us down, I find that it does not account for the rate of weight loss we experience upon ascent. Extremely sensitive gravitometers give weights with such precision that I have been able to predict the depth at which our bodies would be crushed flat by our own weight, and the height at which our weight would be reduced to zero. These vertical boundaries are so close that we are effectively captives of the surface: a matter of only a few times the circumference of the castle."

Marek tried to imagine the limitations that concept imposed upon his picture of the world.

"A mass beneath us great enough to account for surface gravity cannot account for the gradient of weight loss."

"Then the instruments — "

"Have been tested again and again. I can find nothing wrong with them. And unless they render significantly different readings in parts of the world unknown to us, I must accept the figures."

Marek retreated into his own mind. His childhood world had been bounded by the realm of the castle, a playground that offered him room to explore. In adolescence he had been taught about the external forces of nature that impinged upon the castle: forces that evinced a greater reality. From that he made a quantum intellectual jump and realized that much more existed beyond the ramparts than the nearby forest, that the touted stone boundary was imposed not by physical law but by the artifice of tradition. Now Wilam's speculations contradicted Marek's growing vision by imposing borders practically within reach.

"Suppose we dug a deep pit — "

"Or erected a tall tower," Wilam completed. "Yes, I wonder what we would find. Does a dense mass lie just beneath the surface, or — "

Marek's thoughts were suddenly ripped out of his

mind. He plunged from the purely intellectual microcosm of the electronic network into the bitter craw of corporeality. When he focused his attention on the physical milieu, he recognized Charel disengaging the computer connections.

"Is this how the old codger wastes your time when you have useful functions to perform?"

"Sir, I — "

"No excuses, you lazy bondservant. Get out of that computer."

Marek trembled as he unplugged the rest of the body taps. He rose from the console with more speed than care. "Sir, I have completed the duties normally assigned to me — "

"Then you should have reported to me for other work. There is always something that needs to be done — "

"Charel, how dare you burst into my private quarters." Wilam pealed off the wire pads and let the input cables withdraw into their slots. "Your sins become more unpardonable as your power grows more insidious."

Charel ignored the rebuke. "I announced myself at your door — "

"Have you forgotten your computer signature, or do you no longer remember how to tap into the network?"

"I have no need of such antique devices. Scribes manage my correspondence, and domestics, when they are available — " He indicated Marek disparagingly. " — bear messages. You dominate this one's time when a host of menials await your demands."

"You override your authority. My choice of squires is mine to make; nor must I seek your permission to use him as I please. I was a Council member before you were born."

"And one who has spent but little time attending to Council business. Instead, you occupy yourself in the pursuit of knowledge better left unlearned. Do you really think that science is the answer to everything?"

"Your lack of insight is astounding. Science is not

an answer unto itself — it is a prescribed method of deductive reasoning that complements abstract thought. But even if it were only dialectic, its purpose would be served as long as it permitted people to think about the world around them and about their place in it."

"You have always been impious, Wilam, a troublemaker as devious and as deviant as your mate once was; a threat to the community — "

Wilam cut him off. "No, Charel, I do not oppose the people: I resist your authority. I am an aged person, and in my long life I have beheld many changes that frighten me. You struggle to sustain power against a tide of events over which you have no control. You blame the innocent for not enjoying your ignoble prerogative. I seek nothing more than enlightenment, the revelation of truth; that takes nothing away from anyone. If Erbridge writhes in defiance of your ambitions, it is because instability is necessarily short-lived."

"Cease your parables, you senile old recluse! How easily your language obfuscates meaning. I am long past suspecting that you intend to turn your knowledge against me; I know it for a fact. You sway the allegiance of this young apprentice the same way you incite the public: with polished elocution. You would topple tradition without regard for the consequences."

"Ah, poor Charel. I sympathize with your plight. You know that your world is coming to an end and, knowing not how to deal with it, lash out at others in your ignorance and anger. You look for mischief everywhere except at its origin in your mind. If evil has entity, you are its incarnation."

"You cannot trick me, Wilam. I have caught on to your bombastic misdirection. You evade the issues with characteristic insinuations."

"Quite the contrary. I assert only fact while you parry your own prejudication." Wilam ambled awkwardly toward a table full of scientific instruments and fumbled with the dials. He did not succeed in hiding his painful debilities. He convulsed uncontrollably. "If you came here with a motive, I wish you would make it known, and leave me to my devices."

"You enjoy this badinage too much, Wilam. But in the end it will gain you nothing. I will thwart you." Charel followed the elder Council member to his workbench. "Be advised that the Citadel is under siege by rebels and that the palace guards have orders to slay anyone who tries to pass the perimeter."

"Why is this of importance to me? Ill health keeps me quarantined."

"I know about your remote sensing apparatuses. Any attempt to reach them will be met with extreme prejudice. No one is permitted to leave the Citadel — or enter it. That goes for your young convert — "

Marek cringed at the unveiled threat.

" — as well as for anyone attempting to infiltrate our ranks."

"Charel, if only you could comprehend the vacancy of your threats. The world is in crisis, and you worry about minutiae. Carnage will follow regardless of what you do to me or to the people you believe are under your dominion. The mass of scientific evidence predicts it."

"Do not try my patience with your drivel of doom. Erbridge is in a delicate enough balance without your proselytizing. My decree against perimeter passage includes communication as well. Is that clear?"

"Abundantly so. Now leave my chambers and let me rest in peace."

"Heed my warning, Wilam. This is the only notice you will receive. Sedition will meet with severe discipline. And as for Marek — " Charel turned his attention to the apprentice who towered above him. "All loyal subjects are being activated for guard duty. There is insurrection to quell. Already border skirmishes have resulted in death. Pray that you do not find your father at the other end of your pike, because when ordered to kill, you will either do so immediately or suffer that fate yourself."

Marek forced himself to stop trembling. He refused

to be intimidated by one so oppressive. "I will kill if necessary."

"Then we have nothing further to discuss." Charel left.

Marek waited until long after the Councilman's departure before adding, "I will slay him who orders me to commit wrongful murder."

Wilam was laid low by a deep inner throbbing. He eased his body onto a padded sofa and spread himself out for maximum comfort. "Marek, my boy, I fear my time is near. My body torments me more than I can tolerate."

"Do not give up now, my lord. Do not let Charel's malignity drive the life force from you."

"Charel has no control over me, only over my body. And when I can no longer cope with the pain of life perhaps eternal rest is just reward. I am not afraid of leaving this plane of existence, only in leaving so much work undone." Wilam winced. It was a long time before he could continue. "You must carry on that work for me, Marek. You must be here to help Sheena when she returns from her journey."

Marek anguished over his mentor's optimistic belief. He had never met the adventurous daughter, but admired her from afar the same as he admired her mother, for having the courage to tackle the unknown alone and with so little protection. Katha never reappeared. Sheena returned once, but left again at once. Marek knew very little about them. Whenever he and Wilam merged computer circuits, the scientist kept all thoughts of the two women locked behind a stern psychological barrier — like a deep wound too painful to reopen.

"Do you think she still lives?"

"I do not think, I pray. She is our only hope. She must bring back information about our world that will provide some explanation for the increasing catastrophic events, for some way to stave off the ultimate and seemingly inevitable cataclysm. I study effects, but I need more data on the causes.

"My computer studies are stymied by program faults and data loss. I have traced the problem to hardware disruption between the Citadel's terminals and records kept in a remote storage facility. I have explored the backup access routes, but they lead nowhere. The prompts always read the same: file transmission severed. I cannot re-establish the links."

Torment overtook Wilam suddenly. He twisted and contorted into undignified positions.

Marek was more frightened by Wilam's convulsions than by Charel's threats. He touched his master tenderly. "How can I help?"

"Get — get me — to my console. Plug me in. Let me escape this pain-wracked body if only for a while."

Marek dragged the sofa across the room to the computer station. Carefully, he lifted the elder off the soft padding and into the console. He taped the input leads onto Wilam's body, and cringed at the pain he must have inflicted.

"Thank you, Marek. You are as thoughtful as you are loyal."

Marek tapped himself into the computer and opened the direct communication circuits. For a moment he caught Wilam fully exposed; he shared the other's excruciating sores and raw nerve endings. Then Wilam damped the appropriate circuits. Marek lost touch with Wilam's physical perceptions; the scientist was reduced to pure intellect whose lucidity faded in and out in conjunction with the convulsions of his body.

"But what can I do?"

"If only I could find purity, if only I could cleanse my flesh of the sickness that interrupts my concentration. Perhaps if my body were sedated, my mind could roam free in the circuits. I might accomplish more."

"That way lies insanity."

"No. That way lies bliss. I have reached the point at which life is too painful to endure."

"You need body and brain to sustain consciousness."

Entropy

"Yes, my mind is all I have left. Everything I have ever known, everyone I have ever loved, every emotion I have ever felt, these are the sum total of who I am. My mind is all that matters, for it alone can appreciate the true meaning of ecstasy. But enough of hypothetical wanderings; enough of philosophical musings." Between throbs and twinges, he focused his attention on the present. "I burden you with two tasks."

At the speed of an electron, Marek flashed back, "You can depend on me."

"You must keep the way open for Sheena's return, and you must escort her on her next and final journey."

Marek felt tingles of fear deep within his body.

"I have found evidence that the Sacred Portal is more than a myth of antiquity. Whether it is the home of the Ancients or the gateway to the Great Expanse or a massive central processing unit, I know not. But I assure you that in whatever form the Sacred Portal exists, it is the path to life and all knowledge. You must help Sheena find it."

Now Marek felt that he had promised more than he could deliver. Despite his devotion, he swooned at Wilam's charge. Imagining the world outside the castle was one thing; embracing it was another. His fear plunged into a terror so profound that he could not hide it.

"Do not be afraid, my boy. We are so close to extirpation that individual death is only slightly premature. That is why I do not grieve. We have nothing to lose that will not be taken from us shortly. Our insignificant world is caught in the middle of a truly cosmic force, apparently poised between two opposing masses — one below, the other above — tugging at each other. But this struggle is not eternal; it will soon come to an end. And when it does, we end with it.

"Pray, then, that the Ancients did exist, that they knew something that we do not, that they did not abandon us to our fate. For unless they provide a way out of our predicament, we are doomed. And accept the possibility that the Sacred Portal is not a place at all, but a revelation. In that case you may not find life; but it will be more of a comfort to know your fate than to wait for it in ignorance. That is the difference between fact and truth."

Chapter 15

The magic mountains rose in ever-increasing steepness, like the gradient of a sine wave, disappearing into perpetual mist that made the air heavy with moisture. The rock was naked and rough-hewn. Despite the ease of ascent, sheer vertical bluffs blocked the most direct route and forced long lateral detours.

"This be the way." Freder scampered along a broad ledge toward an area where the rock was broken down to body-sized boulders that could be negotiated by short jumps. "It be a hard climb down, but going back up be a cinch. Until we get close to the top."

He did not elaborate.

"I am more concerned about how Charel managed to track us so closely." Sheena bounded effortlessly from boulder to boulder, demonstrating an athletic sense of balance. "This is our second meeting with his retinue — it cannot be a coincidence."

"He was beginning to make sense back there," Marek allowed. "Until he went after you with the knife, I almost believed him."

"He be a bad man, one I care not to have against me."

"You can still escape," Sheena offered. "If you point the way, we can go on alone. Charel's quarrel is with me and Marek, not you."

Freder thought it over. "This all be new to me: sacred quests, times of salvation, people who wield death. I care not for the danger, but the fun of adventure keens me spirit. Besides that, yon friend Charel got me dander up. I think I tag along a bit more."

Sheena vaulted smoothly up the talus. The weight and weariness of extended travel faded with the mounting elevation. "You are either a brave person or a foolhardy one."

The breakdown crested conveniently where a series of narrow ledges began. Freder shoved on without slowing, blazing the trail rather than tagging along. "Brave people live short lives; the foolhardy live not at all. But I believe none of us live much longer unless we stay out of Charel's clutches. From your description, he be a vengeful person, one not to take lightly being pricked by a commoner's bolts."

Marek threw his bulk from ledge to ledge. "And one with a knack for showing up at the wrong time."

"I dislike the person and all he represents. If he be the embodiment of your castle's rulers, I pity your people all the more. He needs to be vanquished even if the world be not on the verge of destruction."

Sheena exhorted, "Have you converted to our cause?"

Again Freder thought before answering. "That the world be going through a major change be obvious. And there be a lot to the world I not understand. These mountains be one of them." Freder scaled a cliff that leaned back at a comfortable angle; the gritty surface was fractured, with enough cracks and crannies to afford ample holds for climbing. "Always in the back of me mind, without knowing why, I have wondered about the structure of the world. Rowed around it many times, I have. The world be flat: a circular landmass surrounded by an infinite sparkling sea, like a leaf in a pond. We row around the land visiting the various coastal castles, and reach our starting point from the other direction. Seems natural.

"Now you come along with a story about the world existing in another dimension, that it be round in a different way: not flat, but curved. Makes no sense. But what does? That the sea goes on and on forever? Never thought much about it. The other side of the sea be somewhere no one ever goes; or if one does, never returns. Course not; takes a long time to return from infinity."

Freder stopped on a ledge below a nearly vertical incline. He seemed disoriented. The fog was dense and practically dripping with moisture. Droplets of condensation clung to the rock surface with very little inclination to fall. Instead of being tear-shaped as drops are at lower elevations, they were nearly round: as if molecular cohesion were stronger than the force of gravity.

"You bend me mind with your tales of walls and force fields, studies of stars and galaxies, renditions of the awesome powers of gravity and magnetism and radiation welling up from underground, and dire predictions of doom. You fill me brain with ideas — uncomfortable ideas. Frightening ideas." After a long pause, "Provocative ideas."

Freder was on a roll that his mind would not let him escape. "Now it be difficult." He ambled along the base of a smooth, monolithic promontory whose top was lost in curling tendrils of fog. The rock ended abruptly at a vertical edge that was a perfect right angle, like the perpendicular cleavage plane of a crystal. Bath surfaces were as slick as the polished facets of a jewel. He started up another rocky breakdown that ran parallel to the line of cliffs.

"Never in all me boating voyages have I passed a swampy shore such as you describe. Erbridge be ringed with castles and sandy beaches. Yet, when I try to reach the opposite sea by crossing overland, I meet a gal who tells me she has been to the end of the world. How be this possible? How be there an end in the middle, a wall of force bisecting the land? The world be curved, she alleges, so the wall be not discernible to the circumnavigator. Sheena, lass, this be less likely than a world surrounded by an infinite sea, and not be explained by an island on a sphere. Your picture of the world be no better than mine, unless your world be half land and half sea. Now the wall.

"We agree that walls have but two purposes: to keep something in, or to keep something out. You suggest we be prisoners. That the Ancients put us here, then erected a barrier to prevent our escape. That we be the subject of some evil experiment? I think not. I think there be something out there we need protection from. And I be afraid to find out what it be."

Marek reeled as he surmounted the breakdown and

leaned against a glazed stone pillar. "Such concepts are as dizzying as these heights."

The crystalline palisades receded into the mist, but leveled off like the approaching crest of a bell curve. The hard rock fractured along planar surfaces that gave the appearance of steps. A stiff wind blew down from the distant peaks.

Sheena felt sick, intoxicated by altitude. The fog swirled randomly, hypnotically. Her weight had decreased so much that she hardly felt the rock ledge supporting her. Itinerant breezes wafted her as if she were the branch of a tree.

She had difficulty focusing her thoughts. "Where — where do we go?"

Freder swayed in the zephyrs. "Up. Always up. Till there be no more up. Then we go down."

Marek leaped up to the next ledge — and kept on going impossibly high. He flailed in fear. Despite his gyrations, his body described a graceful arc that landed him five times farther away than one his size should have been able to jump. He clung for a moment to the edge of a sheer precipice, then levered himself up in a manner that seemed impossible for a creature of mere muscle.

In her dull state, Sheena wondered if she had indeed witnessed the strange spectacle. She hopped lightly after her companion. Once in the air, she found herself propelled by more force than she thought she had exerted. She flew completely over the ledge on which she intended to alight, and crashed against the next ledge above. Her armor scraped painfully over the sharp corner. Slowly she regained her senses. "What is happening?"

Freder crawled sluggishly, never losing touch with the slick surface. "It be the magic of the mountains."

"Antigravity?" Marek was incredulous.

"Magic," Freder repeated.

Sheena slumped in order to maintain her equilibrium. "There must be a logical explana — " She was cut off by something that whizzed by from below. A moment

Entropy

later, a pike grazed the rock next to her, ricocheted outward and upward, reached the height of its trajectory, and fell agonizingly slowly, turning end over end, until it faded into the fog bank. "Charel!"

A vanguard clattered up the ledges just below, followed by the main force negotiating the oddly strewn boulders in the breakdown. One guard reached back, took careful aim, and flung his long-shafted pike straight at Sheena. Without the aerodynamic properties of a spear, the pike was a poor weapon for launched offense, especially when thrown by an inexperienced guard. The pike veered to the side and nearly struck the boater.

"Here be reality uncontested." Freder flattened out close to the vertical rise so he was protected from below by the width of the ledge. "We best be off."

Sheena did her best to shrug off a growing nausea. "Lead on, Freder. I will protect our rear."

The boater scrambled up the ledges without completely breaking contact with the slick surface. "Remember now, no jumping."

Marek stayed close behind him, staggering awkwardly. "Everything seems to be spinning."

"It be a spell that will pass."

With exaggerated leisure, waving her sword threateningly, Sheena backed up the narrow shelves more exposed than she liked. But at least she knew when to dodge deadly missiles tossed from below. Two daggers flew by like streaks; both curved away without coming close. One guard, bigger and bolder than most, crouched low and leaped with all his might. He soared completely past Sheena, hit the rock wall in a tumble, and continued rolling upward out of control, dropping his sword in the process. Sheena raced after the numbed guard and dispatched him with a swift stroke of her sword.

Even as she turned, two more guards attacked her with pikes. She hacked one shaft in two, and knocked the wielder off the ledge; he pirouetted in the air, falling so slowly that when he struck an outcrop below the main contingent, he was stunned but unhurt. The other guard was easy prey for one of Sheena's prowess. She ducked under his pike and slipped her sword between the scales of his armor. He was dead before she withdrew her blade.

The vanguard closed on her. The hatchet-like blade of a pike struck her armor a glancing blow even as she slew the piker. Suddenly she was outnumbered. Quickly she spun and retreated uphill. In her wild flight, she moved too fast and lost her grip on the rock; she floundered helplessly in the air, unable to dodge the pikes and daggers being thrown at her. Fortunately, all the weapons arced by her side.

"Sheena!" Maintaining a firm grip on a shallow crevice, Marek reached out and grabbed onto her; he pulled her into the shelter of a projecting overhang. "We have nearly reached the top."

A raucous wind blew down from the summit with all the fury of a gale. The mist flew past in a steady stream.

Although she was still somewhat dazed, the fight had helped her concentration. "I — thank you."

Marek ignored her remark. He clung unsteadily to his perch. "Sheathe your sword. You need to hang on tight." A guard clambered over the ledge with his pike thrust forward. Marek lashed out so hard that the guard was propelled away from the cliff like a toy. He did not fall, but was carried off horizontally by the wind until he disappeared in the distance. "We have hardly any weight at all. There is nothing to keep us on the rocks but our grip."

Sheena allowed herself to be dragged along until they reached a broad plateau whose other side was shrouded in fog. She flattened out on the glossy surface, seeking minor cracks in which to anchor herself. The wind lifted her bodily off the ground.

"Now be the tough part." Freder huddled patiently before her. "If you let go, you be lost." He slithered along the ground like the apods in the swamp.

"Keep flat. Friction be as much help as ducking the wind."

Entropy

Contrary to what Sheena had anticipated, the effect of near weightlessness was not restful at all. Her mind floated as high as her body. The ground seemed to be in a constant spin, twisting sideways.

Marek took the lead and provided a buffer for Freder and Sheena, who crawled along in his lee. "I can hardly move against it."

"It be worse coming from behind. Then you be backing into it. Last time I synchronized cycles before crossing. Safer knowing how long before the reversal. But with Charel's murderous army chasing us, this be the rightful expedient."

Sheena struggled forward not quite certain what Freder meant. He seldom elaborated unless it was absolutely necessary. Her strength waned fast, giving her newfound admiration for the paunchy wanderer. His shape belied his stamina.

Gradually, Sheena felt the muscle strain easing off. She fought back nausea with greater success, but rippling vapor trails made orientation impossible. It was not until she found herself shuffling forward with less restraint that she became aware of the slackening airflow. She bumped into Freder, and halted.

"Turnabout time."

The wind died to nothing, and motes of dust left suddenly without motive force jittered in discordant circles. Sheena felt as if she were hovering slightly above the sleek crystalline surface. The summit plateau spread without relief in all directions, obscured in fog that lay still as a pall. Her disorientation was exaggerated by the sterile landscape.

She shrugged the pack off her back and fumbled to remove the coriolimeter. Either it was broken, or she could not focus her attention: the gauge readings were way out of calibration. "Are we lost?"

Freder pulled himself up to his full height. He was unsteady, but managed to point the way. "I kept me body aligned with the wind. Hurry, now, before it picks up again." He shuffled off like a plant rooted to soil sliding in avalanche.

Sheena forced enough concentration to shove the instrument into the pack and push herself upright. She was horrified when she shot high into the air and soared completely over Marek. Again he reached out and grabbed her, only this time he did not have a firm grip on the ground; he was yanked up and propelled along with her. They pirouetted in a macabre dance until they coasted back to the smooth summit of the mountain.

"No jumping!" Freder reminded them.

Marek and Sheena followed Freder's example, crawling as quickly as possible without losing touch with the ground. Sheena felt so light that she might have been floating in the air. Wisps of fog wafted past her. She felt a faint breeze at her back.

"Hurry. The wind be turning."

The breeze stiffened briskly. The fog rolled by in solid sheets. The perfectly smooth and flat plateau extended featureless in all directions. Sheena felt herself being lifted up like a toy balloon. "I am beginning to believe these mountains really *are* magic."

"Their properties sure stretch me imagination."

"I cannot stay down!" Marek flattened out and scrabbled along the ground. He seemed close to panic.

"We be almost over the brink."

Sheena splayed before the tempest screaming at her back. She was losing the battle against the powerful jet stream. Only the extra resistance of her clothes and armor scraping along the ground saved her from flying off the mountaintop. Then she crawled over a low ledge that offered some protection from the wind.

A pike rattled across the crystal surface and shot out into space right above her. A dagger followed in its wake. She could hardly believe that a palace guard had the audacity to attack under the circumstances. A moment later, a disjointed guard careened by like a fluttering leaf, and soared straight off the mountaintop. Then two more guards tumbled after him.

Sheena clambered farther down until he caught up with Freder and Marek, resting below an overhang and

Entropy

protected from the raging air current. "I think they jumped."

"And caught in the draft. We be safe now. Anyone trying to cross the summit before the wind changes will suffer the same fate. They have to wait for the lull."

"Does it happen often?" Marek wanted to know.

"It be a periodic cycle. Before making me first traverse, I studied the oscillations. Scared I be, not knowing how far to the other side."

"And you profess not to be a brave person?" Sheena rested easily, although she still felt disorientation. "You have challenged an unknown that would make most people tremble. And how do the magic mountains fit into your picture of the world? Did you row past the edge when circling the land?"

"No, they be inside." Freder gathered himself together for the long downhill climb. "Although it befuddles me to understand how."

"Then perhaps you should attend us to the end of our journey, where the riddle must be explained. We can use a plucky person with your resourcefulness when we sail the sparkling sea."

Freder was about to object when curiosity got the better of him. "What be a sail?"

Sheena was not condescending. "It is a method of propelling a boat without physical work. I can sew one from cloth."

"An enchantress you be, but a sorceress too?"

"You must wait to learn for yourself."

Freder wrested over the idea. "In that case, I escort you to the coast. But no farther."

Sheena hid the pleasure of victory. She was gaining appreciation for the boater's simple yearnings. "Do you not wonder what the Sacred Portal means?"

"That be the stuff of dreams, your quest be the stuff of fantasy."

"Survival is not so insubstantial. It is bitter reality." Sheena rapped the rock on which she crouched. "And unless we do something about it, this reality will crumble from under us. We will be swallowed by the Great

Collapse."
> "Perhaps. And perhaps we be spit out again."
> "Do you want to take that chance?"
> "It happened to me once. Why not again?"

Chapter 16
Flashback

Freder shipped his oar in order to take his turn at the tiller. Although he was the nominal skipper of the galley, rotating positions helped relieve the boredom and keep everyone in shape; it was also good for morale. At the moment, with shore and uncertain shoals approaching, he needed to be in a position of command.

"Samel, take the depth line and drop it off the bow."

"Aye, Captain."

The chief officer yielded the stock of wood that was the tiller. He worked his way along the narrow aisle between the rowers, careful to avoid the butts of the oars. The rhythmic motion of the sweeps was monotonous, but necessary; if they got out of synchronization the galley was difficult to steer. Samel lifted the hatch of the forward cargo hold, groped through the equipment box, and pulled out a tangled rope knotted at intervals. Snarled in the weave were tacks, nails, and bits of ironmongery. He was too long pulling out the junk and untwisting the mess. Freder was concerned as the galley carved through the sea toward the sandy coastline. The boat was damaged enough already without grounding and jarring loose the bottom planks.

"Next time store it in the bucket."

The chief officer was pained by the accusation. "Captain, that trip through the maelstrom knocked everything askew."

At that, they were lucky to be alive.

"Reverse oars."

The crew of twenty halted in midsweep, dipped their blades, and pushed. The galley traveled only a few boatlengths before its momentum was checked. Waves slapped against the hull with noticeable irregularity, imparting a sickening motion that Freder had never adapted to in a lifetime at sea.

"I be sorry, Samel. Did not mean to snap at you."

"No problem, Captain." The chief officer went about his work more heartily. Once he had the rope free, he counted off the knots, each a body-length apart, and laid the rope down in a neat coil. He tied a hefty sinker to the nether end, then lowered the rope over the side. "Six knots."

"Let it drag." Freder was the oldest one aboard, and the boater with the most experience. He knew that landing on uncharted shores could be dangerous: wild animals abounded, and were hunted by sweepers that were wilder. "Advance oars."

Ten pairs of rowers pulled in consort. Twenty wooden shafts groaned with the strain. Well-worn blades dripped high above the froth at each forward stroke. Slowly the galley proceeded through the fog-shrouded sea, seeking a safe harbor.

"Five knots."

Freder was afraid that in their present condition they might not make it to the next castle. The crew had suffered horribly and nearly drowned, escaping from the liquid vortex only by sheer strength and good fortune: when the ocean began rotating, the galley was steering away from the outer eddy, and they were able to spin off the edge instead of being sucked down into the swirling maw.

"Four knots."

Freder pulled the tiller tight against his body, forcing the rudder to port. The galley executed a gradual turn that placed the coast on the starboard side, and the length of the hull in the trough. The mist was thinning, but a light spray was whipped off the undulating ocean by the rising wind. Landfall could be tricky.

"Three knots."

The bane of the boatman was a life lived at sea level. The work was hard, the pull of weight constant. The only respite came between voyages during the sojourn in the castles, where those who plied the sparkling sea were always lodged in the highest chambers. Boaters were treated with great respect.

Entropy

"Two knots."

The galley scudded along the coast. Freder was not about to be rushed into beaching his craft. There was bound to be an inlet or river delta that offered smooth water and protection from squalls. He continued to cruise the offshore shallows.

"Two knots, and steady." Samel snubbed the depth line on a chock; the weight dragging on the bottom tugged the rope away from the perpendicular at an angle that the practiced mariner could read. Then he pulled the sounding stick up out of its guide rail. "We be leaking a bit."

The leaks were minor, little more than an inconvenience. Periodically, Freder had to order two rowers to ship their oars so they could bail out the bilge. "Let it be." Much to Freder's regret, the galley continued to wallow.

The coastline was typical: high-grade crystalline sand falling back to short dunes; dense vegetation topping the rise; and beyond, a steamy jungle dominating a landscape that lay crowded under a thick, cloud-filled sky. Aerial critters flitted about the tall trees. It seemed peaceful and, as long as the sweepers were hunting elsewhere, it probably was.

The dragging depth line suddenly went straight. Samel let out more rope. "Three knots."

This was just what Freder wanted. He shoved the tiller out so the galley turned to starboard, then followed the channel close to shore. He maintained a course parallel to the beach until the longed-for opening appeared: a narrow outflow that connected the high-ground swamp with the ocean. The delta teemed with exotic life forms, swimming and gamboling about the galley. In a little while, Freder descried a rocky outcrop presenting a vertical side that was perfect for docking.

"Ship starboard oars."

Ten rowers — four males and six females — hauled in their oars. Freder worked the tiller to counter the effect of the portside rowers. As the galley touched the crystalline wall, Samel tossed a loop over a pointed rock, snubbed the rope around the midship bitt, and warped in the boat.

"Rest oars."

As soon as the hull touched the rock, five people leaped ashore. Bumpers were flipped over the inboard side. In short order the galley was tied with spring lines, and riding easily on the gentle swell.

"Good job, Captain."

"Thank you, Samel." Freder felt his energy reserves suddenly drain. He and the crew needed high ground on which to rest, and time in which to recuperate from their ordeal. But Erbridge was a hostile land not to be taken lightly. "Split the crew, Samel. Take half to reconnoiter yon hills. The rest remain with me to guard the boat."

"Aye, Captain."

The entrance to the cave that drained the upland swamp gaped just upstream. The opening sparkled from crystals that were constantly washed by the reversing tide. The outward flow was placid. In his youth, Freder had paddled alone into the caves in order to satisfy his desire for adventure. He had followed the complicated drainage system through a network of increasingly smaller tunnels as far as his adolescent courage had permitted. With the arrival of adulthood, the sea had called him away from his boyish pursuits, and transported him around the world in an endless quest for new frontiers.

Samel selected his reconnaissance crew by pairs. Male and female boaters always traveled together. In the occupation of the sea, it was the only way to work because companionship made the long voyages bearable. "Crossbows, everyone."

"Be on the alert," Freder warned.

"We be wary, Captain. It be a shame to get beamed down after surviving the impossible."

Those who accompanied Samel had an easy uphill hike. They marched off happy to have been chosen for the exploratory excursion. The ten rowers who stayed

Entropy

with the boat leaned against the gunwales or sprawled on the deck, resting as best they could under the circumstances. Freder kept a sharp vigil.

The tide slacked after a while, and the mooring lines went limp. The galley bobbed ever so gently. When the tide ebbed, the slight strain was barely enough to keep the ropes taut.

Abruptly there came an awful pressure wave that knocked Freder off his perch next to the tiller and flattened him to the deck with the rest of the crew. The air vibrated, and the ground trembled violently. Leaves were shaken off the trees, loose branches fell, clinging vines swayed and were torn apart. Flying creatures were plucked out of the air and slammed hard against the loamy soil. Tree limbs drooped as if pulled down by strings.

The galley was dragged down so deep that water poured over the gunwales, inundating people pinned to the deck by the pressure. The hull grated against the shimmying rock; the bumpers were quickly worn through and the wooden planks were splintered. Freder and the rowers were powerless in the grip of the quake.

The forest was in motion. A landslide swept down the side of the hill, bringing with it dirt and rock and grass and trees and all the wildlife that a moment before had been flying, perching, or creeping. With a tremendous explosion, the ground split asunder. An immense discontinuity cut diagonally across the hillside, opening so wide that it swallowed a large part of the sliding debris. What was leftover spilled across the gap and poured down the slope, into the tethered galley.

Freder was partially smothered by incoming dirt. "Untie — the — moors!" The crew lay as helpless as their captain.

The galley listed heavily with the lopsided weight, and would have sunk at the makeshift dock were it not for the stretched ropes snapping one by one until the boat broke free. As the mass of material splashed into the stream, the boat was propelled sideways by the waves. The galley did not fully recover from the list; it floated dangerously low with barely any freeboard on the starboard side, but the surface of the stream was flattened by the same phenomenon that was nearly submerging the boat.

The pressure ended as quickly and as mysteriously as it began. The ground stopped quaking, but surface soil already set in motion continued to slide down the slope. The rift remained open, devouring everything that was swept into it; the tallest trees disappeared into the bottomless chasm without a trace. The galley wobbled unsteadily.

"Get the pumps going," Freder ordered as soon as he regained his senses. He flexed muscles strained by the unnatural pull of gravity; only with great difficulty could he lift himself off the deck. "Dump that dirt over the side."

The crew, younger and more resilient, jumped to the task. One pair attached siphon hoses to the bilge pumps and cranked the plunger vigorously. Others pitched dirt overboard; galleys did not carry shovels, so they used spare paddle blades. Freder checked the cargo holds thoroughly for leaks and damage; the hull was intact, and no planks were sprung, but most of the caulking had been squeezed out of the grooves.

"Skipper, we be drifting fast."

Freder clambered over the after hatch combing. He was surprised at the change wrought by the quake. The streambed was dry on both sides, exposing the stony banks and stranding marine animals that squirmed and squiggled to get back into their element. An abnormal tide rushed upstream, hauling the galley as if it were a package on a conveyor belt. Air whooshed into the cave entrance with the force of a storm. A wave higher than the galley was descending upon the craft from the ocean.

Freder's observations did not help him comprehend events. "What be happening?"

Usually in the aftermath of a quake, the land settled

Entropy

down, the whirlpools subsided, wildlife returned to normal, people made repairs and went about their business. There were injuries, fatalities, and permanent crustal changes; but streams did not suddenly flow uphill.

Then Freder noticed that the newly-opened rift extended far back through the lush jungle to a point that must intersect with the cavern artery. Realization dawned slowly in his mind: the quake must have opened a fissure between the surface and an underground chamber. The stream was emptying backward and dragging the ocean with it.

Freder grabbed the tiller. "Dunk the oars! Hurry, or we be lost."

The crew leaped to their stations. They dipped their blades and pulled frantically downstream. As the galley accelerated toward the cave entrance, Freder fought to bring the boat around: if it was struck broadside by the mountainous wave it would surely swamp. His only chance to save the boat was to point the bow into the wave and ride over it — and that before the galley was dashed against the rocky cliff above the cave.

The unexpected speed of events obviated Freder's hastily drawn plan: the reversed current was so strong that the galley was dragged into the crystal cavern before the huge comber caught up with it. The force of the frothing, curling wave splattered against the rock wall with shattering violence; while most of its energy was dissipated, the cave was flooded to the ceiling by the roiling ocean.

Stern first, the galley continued its madcap plunge into Erbridge's inner sanctum. Over his back Freder regarded the glittering walls and lofty ceiling rushing past. Without orders, the stunned crew shipped their oars and clung for dear life to the deck fittings; there was nothing they could do to help the situation: they were no longer masters of their fate, but observers of certain catastrophe. They were trapped between the crashing sea and the unknown reaches of the labyrinth.

Freder could think of no action that could belay the ultimate demise. "Pray for forgiveness, and be the Ancients merciful."

The crew repeated the liturgy sorely out of time, "Be the Ancients merciful."

The great tunnel forked into two smaller tubes: one dry, the other the course of a now-raging river. The galley splashed through the rapids without slowing, bypassed the dry passage, and picked up more speed as the river was funneled into the smaller offshoot. The air was pressurized by the chasing wave that corked the entrance of the cave and forced itself up the tube. Freder fathomed that if the galley was not dashed against the wall the next time the tunnel bifurcated, it would be totally inundated. Either way meant death.

As the tunnel curved, the river rose up against the outside bank. The galley scraped along the wall in a shower of sparks. The steel oarlocks were ripped from their mounting brackets; wooden side planks were chewed into splinters; chunks of crystal were torn off the wall and spilled onto the deck.

Freder clung to the tiller for support, and trembled in fear at what was coming. The ceiling let in the sky at the same time the galley pitched over a fall into the great rift opened by the quake. Never had Freder's guts been so knotted. The galley plummeted into the depths, crashed keel-first into a sea of thick goo, and was propelled away by the froth of the cascading torrent. Somehow, despite the shock, the galley remained upright and afloat.

The weight of extreme depth overcame Freder who, like the rest of the crew, was already weak from fatigue. "Hang in their, mates. Where be there life, be there hope." He did not believe it, but a skipper always promoted optimism for the morale of the crew: a duty that came with command.

The broad cavern could have encircled several castles and their grounds, and probably could have floated them, too. The clear, viscous ocean was more solid than liquid, like poured plastic before it coagulated. It

Entropy

took all Freder's waning strength to fan the tiller. The strange underground sea was too dense to make waves, but Freder could feel it welling up beneath the galley like hydraulic fluid in a piston.

The galley was pumped toward the ceiling and the cracked crystalline rift. The sea — the real sea — poured in from one end of the fault line and splashed out across the impermeable underground sea. The boat's timbers were sorely shaken, but the goo on which it rested was too thick to ooze in through loosened joints and fractured planks.

"Get forward!" Freder abandoned the tiller by rolling toward the bow.

Three crewmembers closest to the stern followed his example. They barely cleared the cargo hatch when the after third of the galley was sheered off as the strange fluid forced the rest of the boat up through the bottom of the crack opened by the quake. In a twinkling, the upwelling goo squirted the truncated galley out of the vast grotto. As the goo receded, it left the boat stranded in the middle of a forest far from the sea. The extruded material spread out over the ground and buried the low shrubbery. Almost instantly the goo solidified into a translucent substance harder than stone.

For a long time, Freder was unable to move. His mind was a blur; he could hardly believe he was still alive. "Praise the Ancients, for they have brought us through this time of woe."

"Praise the Ancients," chimed those of the crew with the presence of mind to consider their surroundings. Slowly they stirred, the strong helping the weak. Gradually they gathered themselves together and waited for directions from their skipper.

The galley was cemented in place; it would never move again. The portion that protruded from the adamant was nearly demolished: a sorry excuse for a boat. Sadly, Freder made his decision. He issued the order that no skipper ever wanted to give.

"Abandon boat, mates. Take what you can carry.

Crossbows all." Freder slung his own weapons, then dropped over the side onto the sleek, hard-packed surface; it was not the least bit resilient, but hard as rock. Freder was still checking out the solidified goo when he noticed movement in the trees. "Ahoy, there."

Samel was flabbergasted as he surveyed the remnants of the galley from the edge of the forest unclaimed by the newly formed substance from the depths of the world. The exploring party collected behind him, equally in awe at finding their boat high in the hills when they had only just left it docked in the stream. There were injuries among the exploring party, but all had survived the effects of the quake.

The chief officer finally recovered his senses. "How be you here with the boat, Captain? And what be this strange stuff?"

Freder made his way across the opalescent adamant that in moments had become harder than any rock or crystal he had ever encountered. "We be brought here by the will of the Ancients on the lifeblood of the world." Still shaken, he made no further comment till the crew arrived from the boat. "We rest here for the moment, then be on our way overland to the nearest castle."

He paused, then added. "Always on the land. Always. Me boating days be over."

Chapter 17

The ocean appeared to extend forever, but, disappointing to Sheena, did not sparkle.

A thin mist hovered above the placid, reflective sea, blending with the surface and making it impossible to determine where one began and the other ended. The air was hauntingly still. Rollers washed gently against the beach like a painter's brush on canvas. If there was danger out there, Sheena thought, it did not show at the moment.

"She be alluring, she be," Freder allowed. "Like a pretty lass in the prime of life."

Sheena shrank at the intrusion. She enjoyed being alone on the dunes where the peace and solitude permitted her to slip her guard. "I never knew the ocean could be so captivating."

If Freder noticed her contraction, he ignored it. "Life be different this side of the magic mountains. Got sweepers, of course, and some rogues among the bunch, but they be kept under control. Wild animals be not a problem."

"It seems almost idyllic."

"Used to be, when the land be stable," Freder mused. He shuffled along the crest of a tall dune. "Before me time. Now everything be different. The quakes come and change the contour of the ground. Weird forces plague the world. Unexplainable happenings be commonplace. You be right, Sheena. Erbridge be barely skirting destruction."

Sheena followed him down the sandy slope toward the harbor, where boats floated serenely at their docks. "Have you convinced anyone to help stave that destruction?"

"Support you have, tools and equipment all you want, and any boat that be idle, but rowers none. A voyage across the sparkling sea be a fearsome prospect for any sane person. Certain personal death be more palpable than predicted racial extinction."

After all her arguments, Sheena expected no different. She had inspired the locals with the purpose of her quest as well as with its urgency, but had enticed no one to join her. The people were scared but not scared enough.

Sheena and Freder arrived at the slip where Marek made his final inspection of the refitted galley. A deep keel had been installed in dry dock, and extra caulking had been pounded into the seams. Outriggers made the once-sleek hull appear ponderous, but Sheena had assured the boatpeople that lateral stabilizers would help prevent the craft from overturning in a storm. She had proved that as a little girl when, using a bellows, she propelled her toy rafts across the Citadel fountain.

"How be the boat building business?"

Marek hopped from deck to dock. "Almost as challenging as castle engineering, without the frustration of missing parts. We have enough spare rope, rigging, and shroud to sail thrice around the world — as long as there is wind. Otherwise, Sheena and I will get very strong at the oars."

The boat's single mast was a stripped tree trunk resting upon a base-plate on the keelson, and fixed from swaying by a series of guy lines that ran from the top of the mast to take-up spools arranged along the outside of the hull. One crosstree provided cleats for the sail.

"Ahoy, there."

Down the road from castle Childge came a boatman with a gunnysack over his back and a crossbow swinging by his side.

"Samel!" Freder greeted his longtime companion with a hug. "Did not know you be hereabouts."

"Just arrived, and not a moment too soon." He plopped his travel kit on the pavement and placed the crossbow on top of it, then turned his attention to the travelers from beyond the magic mountains. "You be Sheena, the lass who undertakes to cross the sparkling sea. And you be Marek, her mate."

Sheena changed color. "Yes, I am Sheena." Although flushed with embarrassment, she could not bring herself to correct Samel's assumption of relationship; she was too stunned to establish it properly.

Marek hunched, but made no other acknowledgment. "Freder has recounted some of your exploits."

"Only captain in the world ever steered his boat into a maelstrom and be expelled. He be a charmed man. But to climb the magic mountains and bring back the savior be even more miraculous. So, when it come to me attention that the captain who swore off the sea returns for further punishment, I know he be needing the help of a good first officer. Be there still an oar for me?"

"Samel, you be the best," Freder interceded. "But those who value life stay ashore."

"Life be short in this world, and not much longer on the ground." To Sheena, "Most believe you crazy. I agree. But in a crazy world only crazy people survive. If no oar be left, can I share the tiller with Freder?"

"You could, if he were going with us."

Samel was shocked. "Gossip has it that he be." To Freder, "You be. You must. They be needing your charm."

Freder was slow to comment. "I be holding back me commitment."

"For what? The end of the world?" Samel indicated the horde of people descending from the castle. "They be timid well-wishers with sand for a soul. You be a daring boater who braved the terrors of the sea. Or be there a change since our parting?"

"No change, friend, only the fear that me next whirlpool be me last. Did not want to taint Sheena's mission with me bad reputation. Stow your gear next to mine, below deck." To Sheena, "Me apologies for wavering, but me mind in a dither."

Sheena was too delighted to object to Freder's consistently vacillating resolve. "You have kept your promise, dear friend. You brought us over the magic mountains and led us to the sea. Your obligations go no further."

"True, but a quick death in defiance be more rewarding than a slow death whimpering. Come, Samel. We be off before the crowd bestows praise undeserved for ventures incomplete." Freder picked up his friend's grip and weapon.

"Captain?" Samel was rooted to the spot, pondering the mast and furled sail. "What be a tree doing in the front of the boat?"

"That be an oar that rows against the wind."

Samel made no response or movement; he merely contemplated.

Half the population of Childge arrived to cheer the explorers embarking on their journey to oblivion. They ranged from toddlers to slumped elders. Some were cheerfully ebullient, others sadly restrained. The thousands of swaying bodies caused the quay to tremble. When Sheena found herself the center of attention, she realized why Freder wished to avoid such confrontation. The fanfare was not to her liking.

One ancient matriarch arrived on a motorized cart, so slouched that she formed a nearly shapeless mass. She drove right up to Sheena. Feeble though she was physically, her mind was still astute. "Be you Sheena?"

"I am."

The old crone ruminated for a while. "I be Fara." She paused so long that she appeared to have passed out, or to have drifted onto another train of thought. But when she regained her senses, she was unexpectedly forthright. "You remind me of Katha."

Sheena felt her innards twist into a knot. She could hardly believe the old crone's pronouncement. "Katha?"

The matriarch slipped into catatonia. The throng continued to sway and chant at the foursome's imminent departure. Marek touched Sheena to show his empathy. But Sheena was nearly oblivious to him; she had been vaulted into the past, into the hidden recesses of memory, where a mother's loving touch had meant so much to her.

"Katha?"

Entropy

Finally, the old crone responded intelligibly. "It was in Geraldge that we met, on the other side of the world. She be a wanderer. Wanted to muster a crew to cross the sparkling sea, but could not find any fools. Set out alone, she did, with a tree and a shroud like yours." The matriarch hesitated, leaving Sheena with her mind atwitter. "Never returned. Neither will you."

The old crone's ominous prophesy dampened everyone's spirits. There was a lull in the cheers of the multitude.

For Sheena, this was a revelation. "Mother made it this far — "

Freder steadied her. "No, she embarked from the other side of the world."

"No matter," Marek interjected. "Wilam told me the Sacred Portal lies off all shores equally, that all perpendicular routes across the sparkling sea lead to the same place."

"How be that possible?"

"The Sacred Portal arises from the axis around which the world rotates, like a wheel on the shaft of an axle."

"Nonsense. The whole castle be discussing the shape of the world of late." Freder directed his dialogue at a still-shaken Sheena. "Most think Erbridge be an island, the magic mountains be a circular range within, the swamp you crossed be a central sump, and the force field be a sphere at the peak of a mount in the middle. That be why you went completely around the barrier, why you returned to your castle from the other side. The wall you believe at the end of the world be a concentric focal point, either the abode of the Ancients or the epicenter of evil."

With images of her mother running through her mind, Sheena could hardly concentrate on Freder's graphic rationalization. "No. Erbridge is round and bisected by a force field; the wall at the end of the world conceals more than we know. The landmass girdles the globe; the magic mountains rise along the circumference. When you row around the world you do not pass along the outer shore of an island, but along the coast of a vast circular sea far from the equator. All shores point inward toward the pole."

Samel waved for attention. "Pardon me, friends, for interrupting these digressions, but who be these sword-bearing warriors approaching — "

"Charel!" Marek pointed toward the palace guard contingent swarming down the dunes. "He is upon us."

Sheena put aside her philosophical muses. "Flee while the lead is ours." She spun and raced along the quay and leaped aboard the converted galley, spouting instructions along the way even though no one was yet on the boat. "Shove us off. Freder and Samel, dunk the oars. Marek, hoist the sail." Her dagger severed the mooring lines.

She pushed the boat away from the dock without waiting for compliance to her commands. A befuddled dock crew assisted from shore; the galley moved broadside out of the slip and was nearly out of reach before Marek, Freder, and Samel landed heavily upon the deck.

Samel grabbed an oar and dipped it, but was obviously bewildered by the rush of events. "You be in an awful hurry, Lass."

"And you not know what we be up against." Freder pulled hard on the center oar opposite Samel. The galley moved gently into the channel as the blades dipped in consort. "These be fearsome killers who slay not machines, but people."

There was precious little wind, but Marek hauled on the halyard that raised the yard. "He must have every guard in the palace."

The number of palace guards converging on the quay was more than Sheena thought existed. "If that is true, how does he control the castle?"

"Surely you be mistaken, Freder." Samel's strong back arched in two as he pulled on the oar and propelled the craft toward the narrow inlet. He never missed a stroke despite his exclamation. "It be inconceivable that a person aim shaft or sword at a fellow

Entropy 137

person. Misunderstood intentions often lead to confusion, but — "

There was no doubt about the carnage occurring at the dock. Charel's guards used their swords and pikes indiscriminately, stabbing innocent spectators and batting them out of the way when they did not move as ordered. The old woman Fara was shoved off the dock with her cart. As the butchery proceeded without abandon, the laments of the injured were abundantly clear to all aboard the galley.

Samel was shocked by the slaughter. "How — how be this possible? What kind of people be these who murder their own?"

Pikes flew in the air after the retreating galley but all fell far short of their goal.

"They be bloodthirsty ruffians who seek power that is not theirs to possess — rogues more deadly to Erbridge than uncalibrated sweepers."

Marek hauled the yard to the very top of the mast. The broad sail billowed as it caught a breeze blowing out to sea. Ropes strained in the chocks, and squeaked where they were rove through the blocks in the pulleys. Soon the galley broke into open ocean enveloped in fog. Waves lapped at the wooden hull. The rowers pulled without further comment; Samel was lost in thought — painful thought that showed with contortion.

"Take the tiller," Sheena ordered.

She changed places with Marek so she could alter the angle of the yard to best utilize the wind. She eased up on the starboard rigging while she pulled in the port. Soon the galley luffed along so swiftly that Freder and Samel found rowing useless: their sweeps could not keep up with the speed of the sea passing by the hull; their blades were merely carried along in the backwash.

"Ship oars, me friend."

"Aye, captain." Samel pulled the oar out of the thole pins and laid the long shaft along the gunwale. He surveyed with interest the swelled sail and the dual outriggers with their sealed pontoons. "This be the strangest boat I ever did row. It moves without effort."

Freder relieved Marek at his post. "Let me take a turn at the tiller, Son. You be piloting us all over the ocean." He took a firm grip on the shaft and played it slowly back and forth. "Steady as it goes, Son. Got to concentrate so as not to over steer." He gave Marek a demonstration, then returned the shaft. "Now give it a try. Slow easy motions. You catch on like you did with the crossbow."

"Captain, we be leaving the shallows and entering the sparkling zone." To Sheena, "The edge of the unknown that wise boatmen skirt. Beyond there be no way to reckon a course."

The all-encompassing fog lay like a pall, and the ocean was confused by a short chop. To Sheena's surprise, the sea did indeed sparkle. Far beneath the fluid surface, discrete energy quanta scintillated hypnotically, like the flickering of a multifaceted jewel spinning on a string. She felt as if the faraway bottom contained the very core of creation, or the means of ultimate destruction. Perhaps both, inextricably intertwined.

"Let this be our guide." Sheena placed the coriolimeter on the deck forward of the tiller. "It has brought me halfway across the world, it will take us the rest of the way."

Samel appeared only partly relieved by Sheena's confidence. "No objection meant, Lass. Only advice. I be here to follow me captain's lead and offer you support. A mateless rower has no obligations but those he chooses."

"Thank you for your confidence, Samel. We may need all the help we can get before this voyage is over."

Beneath the galley the sea sparkled with infinite depth and variety never-ending: a kaleidoscope rotated by immense cosmic forces. Plankton floated idly on the surface in the constant crosscurrent, and larger marine animals swam by oblivious to the speeding boat. Sheena changed the angle of the yard as the direction of the wind shifted. She had much to learn about sailing full-sized craft, but experimentation and the advice of two experienced boat handlers soon led to a collec-

Entropy

tive understanding of this novel mode of oceanic transport.

After a while, the spirit of adventure ebbed into routine. They alternated turns at the tiller and the sail, they performed simple maintenance tasks, and they speculated on the condition of the world as well as its fate. There was ample time for argument and plenty leftover. Only the gravity of the situation preyed upon their ability to rest.

"The drift be always the same in relation to land," Freder explained. "Like a circular treadmill. All boats row around the world with the current."

"If a boat be spun by a whirlpool and the rowers be disoriented," Samel added, "and the bottom be beyond the reach of the depth line, there be no way of knowing whether one be rowing toward shore or into infinity. We be following the route of many a wayward boater who be wandering forever the unknown reaches of the sea."

"I begin to understand why traffic hugs the coast." Then curiosity got the better of her. "But if you believe that, why did you volunteer for this voyage to nowhere?"

Samel reflected for a moment before answering. "Them that got lost without volition knew not whither they be going. It be different for we because we be going there purposely."

The chief officer's dialectics made no sense to Sheena. His convictions were as strong as hers but did not suffer from the anticipation of improper outcome. The difference between a natural-born follower and a self-appointed leader, she supposed, was that the latter expected specific results from her actions. Samel was confident that they were going nowhere, Sheena was afraid they might be.

Time passed.

They kept the galley boatshape. The bilge was pumped dry, drippy seams were caulked, the weather-beaten edges of the sail were stitched, loose planks were nailed. But mostly, time hung loose.

The sparkling sea sparkled. The fog lay thick.

Winds came and went. Sheena began to have her doubts, to lose her sense of purpose. Reality became totally subjective, and Erbridge a place in her mind a long way off. The concept of Universe and the vastness of space took on new meaning — and at the same time became meaningless. She was a mote of dust challenging a storm's right of way.

Then came the awful pressure she knew too well.

The sea flattened in an instant. The air grew denser. The four adventurers were dragged down to the deck and splayed helplessly. Marek for once did not quote the obvious. How long the heaviness lasted Sheena could not tell, for her mind seemed as compressed as her body by the concentrated force of gravity. She was crushed under her own weight.

The ocean exploded downward with abrupt tectonic violence. The galley pitched wildly and settled by the stern, then sideslipped sickeningly. Sheena's insides were pulled in countless directions; she felt as if she were coming apart.

The pressure eased, but the spinning did not. Sheena pulled herself together and slowly comprehended what was happening. The ocean was no longer level. The surface against which the galley floated was tilted sharply and rotating madly like the inside of a gyrating funnel. The boat spiraled down the interior of a mighty vortex.

"We be lost!" Samel lamented. "We be inside a maelstrom that be sucking us down to oblivion!" The chief officer's despair did not stop him from fighting for his life. He grabbed the central starboard oar and pulled frantically. "Freder, dip your blade and row us out of here."

The captain followed suit. "Pull for your life, Lad. Pull!"

Along with the whirling sea came a cyclonic wind. Sheena and Marek struggled with the yardarm ropes, and tightened the lines on the sail whose corners flapped wildly. They got the canvas under control and before the wind. The combined efforts of oar and sail

Entropy

slowed the galley's slide down the inclined plane, but could not lift it up against the normal pull of gravity.

"It is not enough!" Marek exhorted.

The spout at the base of the funnel was filled with a brilliant white light that neither spun nor sparkled. It simply existed. With each rotation the galley descended farther down the slope, drawn inexorably toward the bottomless hole in the middle.

"We are too heavy. We need to get rid of some mass." Sheena tore off the forward hatch cover and threw it overboard. "Marek, help me dump the stowage."

The mast creaked and groaned, straining the stays almost to the breaking point. The yard jolted with the gusts while the sail fluttered furiously. Marek wrapped the bitter end around a belaying pin. Together, he and Sheena threw over the side their weapons, instruments, supplies, spare sails and rope, and all unnecessary equipment. With the hold empty, the galley held its own in the mammoth eddy, but would not climb the gradient.

"It be not enough!" Freder threw his back into each stroke. "It be closing up around us."

Marek was barely able to withhold his panic. "Let us unload the after compartment."

Sheena thought hard and fast. "Better yet, let us cut it free." She yanked the toolbox from the forepeak locker, took out axes and saws. "Start chopping. All of you."

She set the example by running the saw blade through the rail between the mast and the center thwart. Marek hacked with such energy and strength that wood splinters and planks appeared to explode off the hull. Freder and Samel let go the midboat oars and climbed up the steeply tilted deck.

"Aft of the forward bulkhead!" Freder warned.

The hull was divided into four sections by transverse bulkheads as proof against flooding, a design that ensured that the galley would remain afloat despite any completely flooded compartment.

Once the others were at work, Sheena clambered down the starboard rail and sawed through the after outrigger stanchions. She was so dizzy from the rapid rotation that she had difficulty concentrating, as if her brain were at the end of a flywheel. Valiantly, she fought off vertigo, and retained enough presence of mind to scoop up the coriolimeter. She sawed off the port outrigger stanchion, then scaled the port rail to the bow. The pontoons were cut free from the stern of the galley, but still connected by the forward stanchions.

By this time the deck was sawdust, and the other three were chopping through the pillar and support brackets. Swinging with a will, Marek quickly hewed through the starboard strake, futtock, and planking as if they were grass instead of seasoned wood. When he reached the wale, the galley split abruptly right down to the keel.

Both Freder and Samel dropped below and chopped at the main structural member until it broke in two. The after two-thirds of the galley was suddenly twisted sideways by the intensified spin at the lower end of the vortex. As it dropped, it revolved faster and faster, spiraling into the unwavering white light until it was completely engulfed by the reverential luminary. It was gone in a flash.

With less weight and drag, the sail captured enough wind to haul the truncated fore section up the incline. The boat's lateral motion slowed as it approached the crest of the whirlpool. Then it was spun off at a tangent.

"Lower the yard, Marek!"

As Marek loosened the halyard, Sheena struggled to pull in the bottom of the sail. The design faults of the crudely constructed sailboat were accentuated by the absence of its long sleek hull. Without the stern section to counterbalance the power of the wind, the bow dipped sharply into the waves. The boat yawed randomly with no tiller. The deep keel was also missing, leaving only the outriggers to keep the galley upright; the forward stanchions groaned with the additional stress.

Entropy

Freder and Samel lashed together two pairs of forward oars, and made double makeshift tillers which they hung over each side and braced against the gunwales. With side-sweeping motions they helped stabilize the galley's weaving course. Sheena sailed tight into the wind with very little sail, thus reducing the pitch. Marek nailed extra braces to the outrigger stanchions. Thus they managed to maintain moderate control of what remained of their frail craft.

They remained at their posts despite the exhaustion of their ordeal. Theirs was a life or death struggle not just for themselves, but for the world. They continued to sail across the current in the direction indicated by the coriolimeter. Eventually, the sea stopped sparkling. Samel tossed the depth line and hit bottom. Out of the fog loomed an oddly formed strand and broken, unrepaired docks.

Dense shrubbery dug roots into the nearby dunes, tall trees dominated an alpine landscape, the forest was replete with critters that took no notice of the immigrants. It could very well have been the same stretch of coast they left so long ago. Only the battered instruments and faith in her indomitable will to succeed led Sheena to believe they had prevailed in crossing the sparkling sea to the land of the Sacred Portal.

She ran the wobbling boat onto the beach. When the keel grounded, the galley lurched over onto its port side and snapped the outrigger stanchion. Waves gently washed at the jagged edge where the hull had been lopped off. Like the dead, they stumbled ashore.

"Praise be the Ancients," Freder and Samel chanted together as they fell prone on the crystalline sand.

Marek collapsed in a heap, too weak for comment.

Sheena squatted fitfully. Although her body ached with fatigue, she wanted to continue. She did not yet feel the throb of triumph. The sparkling sea was a minor obstacle, a physical hindrance well within her grasp to conquer. Now came a much more difficult passage.

The worst was yet to come.

Chapter 18
Flashback

Sheena sneaked with ease through the Citadel's underground barricades, but once inside found that the cathedral-like lobby and central ramp were crowded with guards and civilian errand runners all scurrying about in Brownian motion. Mass confusion reigned.

Since she wanted to reach her father's lofty chamber without making her presence known, she ducked into the service ramp that wound like a helix within the walls. Only servants used the enclosed ramp, but none of them paid any attention to the ragged warrior returning from her historic trek around the world. They were all too busy doing the Council's bidding.

Once in the upper levels, she took out-of-the-way corridors in order to avoid roving sentinels. She ducked into empty rooms and storage closets whenever a guard came too close. Then she found a pile of soiled clothes in a hamper, and donned the dress of a chambermaid over her armor and travel wear. Soon she slipped unnoticed into her father's private quarters.

Wilam was in such pitiful condition that Sheena was immediately overcome with despair. He lay flat before his computer console, seeming more dead than alive. He moved hardly at all: a slight palpitation that was more nervous quiver or electric stimulus than the beat of life. The input terminals attached to his body plugged his consciousness into the data banks.

Sheena fell on top of him, cradling him, cuddling him. He was the only part of this uncertain world that she loved. "Father! Father! Are you there?" She shook him, gently at first, then hard. He did not respond, seemingly unaware of anything occurring in the physical world extrinsic to the chemical flow within the cells of his brain and the synaptic connection to the electronic passage of data. She did not know if he was even capable of anatomical response.

Entropy

Desperate to communicate with him, she plugged herself into the computer and quickly activated his access code.

He came on line at once. "Sheena, my baby, what are you doing in this program?"

"Father, I am not a program. I am alive."

"Alive? Nonsense. You are a construct. I wrote you myself."

Now Sheena was gripped with fear, for she recognized the near-death condition of willing assimilation into the computer's electronic circuitry. "Father, you did not write me," she pleaded. "You sired me. You and Katha. Or have you forgotten her as well?"

"I forget nothing. I am incapable of forgetting, except temporarily, when my circuits are overloaded and my data circle through feedback loops. But my retrieval programs run perfectly." Electrons spun a few million times around their nuclei as Wilam searched his memory. "Ah, the name is familiar. Katha was an associate programmer, was she not?"

"She was my mother. Your mate. I am the result of your meld."

"Sheena, there is a glitch in your programming. You express ideas that are part of an artificial world I am writing in my spare time: a place where plants grow and animals prowl, absorbing sustenance from the air instead of drawing electricity from the ground; where people live tenuously in castles; where the past has been forgotten and the future is uncertain; where time and space come together; where — "

"Father! Stop! You are describing the real world — the world of which your body is still a part. You are not a computer. You are Wilam. And I am your daughter, Sheena, your own flesh and blood, returned from a journey around the world. An exploratory trek on which you sent me."

"How can that be? I am still writing the program. I have not yet worked out all the laws and dimensions, I have not yet correlated all the data. I am missing mathematical proofs, and stymied by logic faults — "

"Father, I have the data you need to complete your calculations. I got them from a scientist like yourself, from the computer of another castle. She had access to undamaged files that were stored in a magnetically proofed vault built by the Ancients; files filled with concepts only you can comprehend. But Father, I must have your attention — "

Sheena pulled one of the plugs connecting Wilam's mind to the computer. Static flooded his circuits, creating electronic convulsions that were the computer equivalent of muscle spasms. Some of Wilam's thought processes were sucked out of his programs; it was like stripping flesh from muscle. He seethed in mental agony.

"Sheena, what are you doing — "

"I am saving you, Father. I am bringing you back to reality."

"You are — you are killing me." Wilam struggled mentally. "I cannot live in this body — "

The anguish she inflicted upon him hurt Sheena almost more than she could bear. But she had to get him out of the computer at all costs. "It is for your own good." She disengaged another lead.

Wilam's body writhed.

"Please come to me, Father. I need you."

"Sheena, I — ah, the pain — Sheena, do not put me back in my body. I cannot take it — oh, Sheena, my baby, I am sorry — I have been locked up so long — the pain — it is the only thing that reminds me that I have a vital force of my own. I have missed you so much — aaagh — my daughter, you have been gone so long I gave you up for lost — aaaaggghh — "

She reconnected one of the terminals. "Is that better, Father? Are you all right now?"

Wilam's mind sought programs to protect him from anguish, to subdue the raw pain assailing nerve endings gone awry. With long enough circuitry, he was able to escape the constant agony with which his body was inflicted. "I am — yes — that feels better. I — " He was conscious again of himself, of who he was: not a

Entropy

machine but a living organism. "Sheena, my daughter. You have brought me back from the edge of oblivion."

"And the pain?"

"Your love is my comfort."

Electrons continued to flow while father and daughter expressed their love for each other. Then came the hard return to reality.

She caressed his nearly shapeless body. "I am sad to find you — this way."

"Sheena, my baby, do not grieve for me. I do not have much longer to live in this world — no one does. But of my dissolution I have no fear. Often of late I have sought such release. Only thoughts of you prevented me from letting go."

"Father, do not even think of such — "

"I must, my baby, for we must all return to the ground from which we have sprung. That is the way of nature. My pain now is that you must so soon be on your way."

"Father! How can I leave you now — "

"Because you have no choice. Your life, as well as the life of the world, hinges upon events only you can effectuate. The palace guards have orders to kill you should you ever return, as a lesson to the proletariat who would foment insurrection. The Council does not understand the concept of martyrdom. But some are on my side; they, I hope, will save the castle. But unless you find the Sacred Portal and unravel its secrets, Erbridge is doomed to destruction. The Ancients meant for us to do this."

"Father, how do you know? How can you be so certain — "

"Because I have reopened many closed programs since you departed. I have learned a great deal about our world. And although I do not understand exactly what is happening, I know for a certainty what will occur. I know that our lives and the lives of our ancestors will have been useless unless we change the course of the world."

Sheena did not want to accept his rationale, but

knew in her soul that she must. All her life had been spent in the pursuit of one goal: survival. Now more than ever she needed strength and inner resolve. Begrudgingly, she accepted the hard return to reality. She input an outline of her observations, as well as the transfile from Grange.

Wilam ruminated over the raw data for a long, long time. Sheena pointed out the most important features: her measurements, and Prissa's esoteric studies. Wilam became more mentally alert.

"It makes sense. It all fits together. There are access codes that I never knew existed. They will lead me directly into the same data bank that Prissa accessed. They were once all connected. Perhaps they can be reconnected — all the castles relinked, sharing all their resources — "

Sheena was not completely integrated into the computer. Because she kept part of her mind monitoring sensory input, she was not caught completely unawares when Boram broke unannounced into Wilam's chamber. She disconnected herself, but her reaction time was slow: by the time she yanked out her sword and barely parried Boram's blade, he had slashed at the input cables and severed three of Wilam's leads. The aged scientist retched with pain as his mental contact was cut from the computer.

"You have no right to be here, Sheena."

She leaped out of the console with her sword leading the charge. She could have killed him on the spot had not the chambermaid's dress hampered her draw. "It is you who act without right. This is my father's chamber."

Swords clanged loudly as steel met steel in deadly combat. Boram backed from the terrible onslaught. "Wilam is under arrest. The Council has deemed his wild ideas a threat to the community."

A parry, a feint, a roundhouse lunge, and Sheena nicked the plates of her opponent's armor. "You are good, Boram. You have been practicing."

Boram cringed along the crystalline partitions, his

brute force tactic yielding constantly to her superior skill with the blade. "We do not need to fight. We can go far together. It does not have to end this way."

"Sarcastic sentiment for one who sends greetings with a sword."

"I meant only to get your attention."

She slashed hard and fast, trying to get under his guard. "You did."

Boram was on the defensive but showed no fear. "Be reasonable, Sheena. We can rule Erbridge together when our time is due."

"Our time will never be due."

They battled completely around the room, Boram ceding ground and Sheena giving no quarter. He managed to stay alive by meeting each thrust with a parry. Furniture, fittings, and dusty instruments were battered and knocked askew in the brawl.

Sheena, who had never wished death upon a living soul, tried her best to slay the one who gave no thought about her father's delicate condition.

"Stay your anger, Sheena, and be reasonable." While retreating from her sword, Boram worked his way back toward the computer console. "We can work this out. Trust me."

"There is only one end to this, Boram."

Wilam's sagging body shuddered. "Get away while you can, my baby. Get away." He was collapsing fast, but mustered the strength to plead. "If he kills you, he kills us all."

"No one has to die!" Boram did not stop swinging his blade; he could not, or Sheena would have cleaved him in two. "But the people must not learn of your heresies."

Sword-bearing guards flooded into the room. Sheena spun in a roundhouse sweep that kept them at bay. Boram took advantage of the respite to slash through the remaining computer cables.

Wilam went instantly still.

"You beast!" Sheena advanced upon the provost marshal, but before she made a stroke, found herself besieged from behind by the guard contingent. Only her back armor saved her from instant death. She fought now on all sides, beating back the guards despite their numbers. They were innocent babes in battle, their swords no more effective than rattles.

"Get away, Sheena! Get away! You must find the Sacred Portal. You must. It is our only salvation." The great scientist went limp. Then, weakly, "It is your destiny."

With pangs of remorse, Sheena realized that her position here was untenable. She could not help her father by dying before him. Logic took control of her emotions. In a bold charge, she burst through the guards between her and the door, breaking into the corridor beyond. No one could best her in single combat; no one could halt her escape from the castle. Against the poorly trained palace guards, she was invincible.

She raced down the grand ramp with Wilam's brief and final eulogy lingering in her mind, and emptiness in her heart.

Chapter 19

The crossbow thwacked. The wooden bolt sped over the sandy beach toward the tree line. Then came a clang, a sizzle, a burst of sparks, an explosion, and a shower of metallic debris.

"Good shot, me lad."

Freder cautiously approached the dying sweeper. His own crossbow was wound and an arrow was notched; the steel-tipped point was aimed unswervingly at the shiny, upended ball. Eight pincerlike legs twitched randomly as stray electric discharges plagued shattered circuit boards.

"The lad be deadly with a bow," Samel agreed.

"Another one is coming," Sheena warned. She pulled her instrument pack out of the wreckage of the galley, and slung it over her back. She did not bother to draw her sword.

"May I take this one out, too?" Marek, his confidence obviously bolstered by the effectiveness of Freder's training and by the accuracy of his first bolt released in defense, quickly spun the crank and notched another arrow.

"This be not a game, me lad." Freder hugged the ground and waited for the next sweeper to emerge from the dense underbrush that tangled the forest floor. He motioned to his fellow boatman. "Samel, over there."

The chief officer took a position next to the bole of a huge tree. His crossbow was primed and ready. "It might be not rogue."

"Take no chances in a hostile land."

Marek hunkered down behind a low dune. Wind-blown sand had covered most of the ancient seaport. He appeared unperturbed by either Freder's caution or the imminent duel. Before him lay a paved clearing; on the other side, a road carved a straight line through the woods. Thick mist hung in the air.

Sheena quit the beach and took cover next to

Marek. "I counted upon mechanical sentries blocking the path to the Sacred Portal, but I did not expect to be engaged so soon after our arrival."

"This quest has been full of surprises."

The ground rumbled. A deep vibration was transmitted to Sheena's flattened body. This was not the onset of a quake for there was no accompanying pressure. Something large rattled toward them along the fog-shrouded road. As usual when she faced the unknown, Sheena unsheathed her sword. She issued a low warning to her companions. "Steady."

Three crossbows were trained on the oncoming apparition slowly taking shape through the haze. It was rectangular, the size of a large room, and sleek despite bulbous sponsons along its front and sides. It rolled on two steel treads made of linked squares. Half the top was fitted with shallow depressions; the back half was an open compartment. The tracked machine paused in the clearing and idled its motor.

"It be a conveyance," Samel exclaimed with delight from his position in hiding. "Come to take us lickety-split to the Sacred Portal."

"Wait!" Sheena held the overexuberant boatman from exposing himself. "Let us make no assumptions."

She slithered across the sand to a point halfway between Marek and Samel. Freder stayed on full alert on the other side of Marek. Sheena gradually displayed her body above the embankment.

The machine hummed. The forward sponson parted in the middle to reveal an array of sensors, antennas, and unrecognizable devices. One whirling loop antenna moved out on a rod that bent and homed in on Sheena. When the entire machine pivoted by spinning its tracks in opposed directions, her innards gripped tight with fear, but she maintained her stance. The machine deployed two hinged ramps, one from either side: an open invitation to climb to the topside resting depressions.

"By the grace of the Ancients." Freder pulled himself upright and lowered his crossbow. "You be right,

Entropy

Samel."

A moment later the six lateral sponsons snapped open. Discharge nodes poked through narrow slits and fired at their targets. Freder ducked and rolled, while Sheena dropped flat to the ground. The sand in front of her burst into globules of molten silicon, splattering her dress and armor.

Both Marek and Samel shot their crossbows. Marek's arrow flew straight toward a sponson, but was deflected by a quickly closing shutter. Samel's bolt hit the hull and bounced off like a rubber ball.

"It be armored."

The treads clanked, the mighty machine pivoted. The ramps were retracted halfway, then set out again. Retaliatory fire was concentrated upon the two crossbow wielders busy reloading. Marek twisted aside in time, but Samel was singed by a near miss; he rubbed his smoking clothes in the sand.

Freder fired a bolt that ricocheted off the tread guard. "That be a confused machine."

"Its programs have probably been deranged by the same magnetic fluxes that confuse the sweepers." Sheena crouched behind the dune feeling helpless with only a sword and a dagger for offense. "It does not know whether we are to be transported or liquidated, so it tries to do both."

Everyone stayed hidden. The guns fired haphazardly where the sensors had last ascertained targets. One ramp unfolded, the other closed. The rear gate dropped to the ground on a slant.

"Now it wants freight." Frustrated, Freder turned to Sheena for direction. "What be your notion, Lass?"

"Knock out its sensors."

Marek poked his crossbow over the top of the dune, aimed, pulled the trigger, and fell back from the blast already coming his way. His quiver was holed. "There is nothing wrong with its reaction time."

The machine rolled forward with guns blazing. The three with crossbows scampered away below the crest of the dune, but Sheena stayed her ground.

"Draw its fire!"

That was being done without her recommendation. Energy beams nipped at the crossbow wielders as they flanked the paved clearing and leaped for protection into the forest. Before Sheena knew what was happening, the monstrous machine rolled off the edge of the pavement right over her; she was straddled by the broad tracks. The guns enfiladed the ocean side of the dune, but its targets had already escaped.

Sheena was nearly crushed under the heavy weight of the rear gate dragging behind the machine. Only by scudding along beneath the bristled undercarriage did she avoid being flattened permanently. Steel-tipped arrows darted out of the forest and clanged against the armored hull. One gun ceased firing. The machine swiveled completely about on its axis, affording Sheena enough time to crawl out from under its forefront where she was out of range of the side-mounted guns.

She slashed her sword across the open instrument panel, sheering off antennas, slicing wires, and demolishing delicate sensors. Electrical shorts flared, nicking and blackening her sharply honed blade. She had time for a single backslash before the motor throttled up and the machine lurched forward. She could not escape to the side because of the fear of being gunned down. Again the machine ran her over, but this time she grabbed onto the soft, rounded bristles and allowed herself to be dragged across the pavement.

The machine was still behaving erratically. With its sensors incapacitated, its gunfire was ineffective; it blasted quite a few trees and burned a lot of grass before its guns shut down completely. The side ramps flapped in and out. The throttle raced and slowed, causing the machine to drive haltingly along the road. The rear gate lifted.

Sheena let go. She rolled with the forward momentum, stopped, and scuttled out behind the machine under the partially closed rear gate. Then she lay flat on the ground, unmoving, while the machine retreated into the fog. When it was gone, the crossbow wielders

Entropy

emerged from hiding.

"Are you all right?" Marek's concern was evident by his embrace. "Yes, I — I am fine."

"That be quite a trick," Freder exclaimed. "A bold lass with bold ideas." Sheena did not feel as confident as she appeared. "My actions were unplanned. I was overtaken by events."

"I think the machine be outwitted by a fair lass slight of frame." Samel picked up her dropped sword and slid it into her back-scabbard. "A stunning brain with a body to match."

Sheena concealed her embarrassment with action. "Come. Let us be on our way."

Marek released her and reached for the instrument pack. "Let me get out the coriolimeter."

"We do not need it."

"But where do we go?"

"Along the road, of course. That machine was originally programmed to transport people and packages arriving from across the sea. The defensive armament must have been for use against wild beasts encountered on its route — efficiency through double duty. I think it will lead us someplace we want to go."

"Worse than bold. Daft." Freder shrugged, reloaded his crossbow. "I be, too, for getting meself into this mess." Despite his sentiments, he took the lead. "But would not miss it for the world."

Marek also reloaded his crossbow, and carried it at the ready. "What kind of beasts demands the protection of six guns?"

"Big ones."

The road ran as straight as the blade of a sword. It crossed no intersections, it met no side streets, it passed no buildings. It simply went on interminably, a clear path through an otherwise dense forest of towering trees, drooping vines, and a thick undergrowth of wiry weeds. The wilderness was alive with animals, but none that seemed belligerent. Strangely plumed creatures swooped down occasionally from the sky, flapping elongated wings that ended in grasping digits. The proliferation of small ground critters that dashed alongside the road appeared curious rather than dangerous.

"Be there any legends from your castle that describe the Sacred Portal?"

"Only that it is the ramp to salvation," Sheena replied.

"We be on the rise," Samel noted. "Gradual, but sure."

"Wilam was certain we would recognize it when we found it," Marek added. "And that we could not miss it when we got there because all roads lead to it, and nothing exists beyond it."

The road went on and on. No wild animals charged, no rogue machines attacked. Creatures skipped, skittered, and glided through the air, either unaware of the four intruders or unconcerned about them. The diminishing weight and the lack of stress made the land idyllic for traveling.

"None of these upland animals have defensive appendages," Marek commented. "And the only sweeper we encountered was on the beach, beaming those clawed things climbing out of the sea."

"It be too good for truth." After a while, Freder unloaded his crossbow and slung it over his back. "Our souls be needing salvation even if we die from boredom."

Sheena examined the trees and bushes growing up to the very edge of the road. "Notice how clean the paved surface is, and how evenly cropped are the bushes that border it?"

Marek stopped for closer scrutiny. "The ends of these branches have been — burned off."

"I think the carriage machine sweeps the road with its brushes and trims encroaching plant life. An innocuous occupation when functioning properly."

Samel showed more disgust than interest. "Nothing in this world be working like it should."

The forest thinned as the elevation increased, and the scrub brush thickened. Legions of small, furred animals gamboled about in the grass. The air was still, and the light mist hung in distinct layers. The road in front was a conic clearing whose end was lost in perspective.

"I feel a bit dizzy," Marek complained. "Like I did near the top of the magic mountains. Mind and body are nearly afloat."

"I be dizzy, too," Freder confessed. "Something be moving before us, and it be a tree."

"By the Ancients, you be right."

Quizzical at first, Sheena motioned for them to stop. "You are correct, at that."

The tree was not falling, it was moving slowly crosswise in an upright position, past the discernible opening in the forest made by the road. Then like a phantom it was gone.

"Me senses be deceiving me."

Another tree separated from the forest and traveled slowly across the road in the distance. Then there were two together. More passed, in ones and twos; then came an entire grove that temporarily blocked the road.

"If that is true, we are all deceived." Sheena advanced without restraint. "Let us proceed. I have never been stalked by a tree. This will be a new experience."

"She be seeking adventure that the sane avoid."

Freder drew his crossbow. "If the trees be hostile, we fight wood with wood."

Bold as she appeared, Sheena did not rush into possible danger. With her sword in front, she led a slow charge toward the parading timber. It soon became apparent that not only trees were on the move, but the entire forest: vines, grass, shrubbery, and all the attendant animal life. Only the mist was static where it hovered above the tree tops; lower down, it was shredded by arboreal motion.

The road came to a tee beyond which lay only a thinned-out forest on a continuous rise. The perpendicular paved surface moved sideways with the woods, acting as a separation zone between the stationary forest and the mobile forest. The road from the sea overhung the intersection; a ramp with rollers extended in either direction, almost touching the grooved road sliding underneath.

"It be a conveyor belt like those in the castles," Freder announced. "Or like the underground highways that no longer work."

Marek could not contain his disbelief. "Broad enough to carry an entire forest?"

"Aye. And strong enough." Samel tested the cantilevered tee-shaped structure with his weight, little as it was. There was no sag. "What be you making of it, Lass?"

Sheena sheathed her sword. "Exploration often leads to the unexpected. In a lifetime of travel, I have repeatedly wondered whether the things I encountered were governed by natural law, or were the result of circumstances created by the Ancients. I suggest we continue. Disregard for now what we do not understand, and worry later about its meaning. If the Sacred Portal is indeed a source of wisdom, it will explain everything."

Samel pointed haughtily. "Perhaps we be taking the road that be coming our way."

Carving a path through the moving forest was a paved surface grooved with the same rectangular configurations as the conveyor belt under the overhang. It approached slowly. For a moment it coincided with the road from the sea, and was practically a continuation of it. Then it passed by and eventually vanished in the distance.

"All roads lead to the Sacred Portal," Marek intoned.

Sheena was startled into immobility. She did her best to mask her bewilderment at this new turn of events. "Behind every legend lies truth disguised."

"And there be times when nothing makes sense but the absurd." Freder joined his fellow boater at the edge of the overhang and leaned out over the underbrush. Small amorphous creatures cringed in the thicket with their tentacles wrapped tightly around the slender branches. They crawled sluggishly, always maintaining a firm grip with one tentacle before letting go with the

Entropy 159

others. "Curious the way they be clinging like that as if they be afraid of being pitched about."

"Notice the size and shape of the grooves, Sheena?" Marek pointed out the indentations in the passing pavement. "It is identical to the tread pattern on the carriage tracks."

Sheena took close observation. "And the spacing is the same."

"Those rollers at the bottom of the ramp must allow the carriage to freewheel onto the roadway where the treads engage the depressions. Coming from the other direction, the carriage can disengage in order to drive up the ramp and turn toward the sea."

"But why?"

"Traction. There must be slippage with the loss of weight."

"Do not be doing the job of the Sacred Portal. Answers be at the end of the road, and another one be coming our way. Be you ready to take the plunge, Samel?"

"After you, captain."

Before Sheena could issue a countermand, they jumped. First Freder, then Samel left the platform in an impossibly long arc that brought them down far off in the bushes. They were rolled sideways by the angular momentum in a succession of bounces that had them whirling uncontrollably in the air, tearing out leaves and small branches, until they grabbed onto limbs substantial enough to hold them. Then they clung for all they were worth, like the tentacled creatures among which they had landed.

"That be fun, Captain. Can we be doing it again?"

Freder seemed too giddy to reply.

"It is as if the top of the world is a spinning disc," Sheena noted wryly. Her mind was befuddled as much by altitude as it was by the impossibility of the situation. "How can that be?"

"I have no doubt that truth will be revealed." Marek hunkered low and sidled down the ramp to the rack of rollers. "There will be less stress if we slide down onto the moving road." He set the example for her. His body skimmed over the rollers with a speed that matched that of the road below; he alit easily without being jerked.

Sheena followed suit. She let the road move Marek out of the way before letting herself go. As she landed on the crosswise road, she instinctively reached out for the rectangular depressions: the world spun about, and she needed something to hang on to for fear of flying off into space. Despite a peculiar lightness, her dizziness soon diminished, and after a while, her perspective reversed itself: she seemed to be stationary while the forest just abandoned was flowing sideways.

"It be like an eddy current along the bank of a river," Freder proclaimed. He and Samel slunk through the underbrush like apods in the swamp. They stopped at the edge of the road, clinging to wiry weeds. "Two currents be passing in opposite directions, each steady as it goes. Only at the juncture be there turmoil."

When Sheena turned toward the boaters, the illusion of movement dissipated. As long as she ignored the world behind her, she could maintain her equilibrium. She wondered: if her brain could be so easily deceived, how about her instrumentation? She pulled out the coriolimeter; it registered zero. "It must be broken." She stuffed it back into her pack.

"Shall we crawl back to that next road?" Marek sidled close to Sheena without letting go of the depressions.

She crept from hole to hole like a living carriage track. Marek stayed right behind her. Freder and Samel elected to make their passage through the underbrush because they thought it was easier to hold on to the vegetation. Sheena refused to acknowledge the presence of the moving forest beside her. When she reached the next road, she turned away from the direction whence they came.

"This way to the Sacred Portal."

They crept onward. Soon the once-motionless now-transiting forest lay far behind, lost in the mist. Indeed,

Entropy

Sheena felt that by crossing that improbable discontinuity, the entire Universe was in back of her, that in front waited a convergence of forces, a pinpoint of reality, a place where time stood still and where space had no meaning.

All that she had experienced in life was but a prelude to this moment of arrival, to the ordeal that was yet to come. She had strength, stamina, and will power — enough to overcome any obstacle in her way. But for the first time in memory, she felt doubt. Deep inside she knew that the toughest barrier she must overcome now was not physical, but conceptual.

Chapter 20

Flashback

When Marek entered Wilam's chamber, the senior scientist was closer to death than to life. Having the electrodes ripped off his body had snapped him back to painful reality with such high impedance that, in his weakened condition, there was little chance of survival without extreme medical attention amounting to total organic function management.

Unable to obtain a response, Marek connected the secondary input leads to Wilam's body and let his mind trickle back into the computer. Then he found a set of spares and plugged himself in as well.

"Hello, my boy."

"Wilam!" Marek was ecstatic that his sage and mentor was able to maintain electronic consciousness within the computer network. "How are — are you all right?"

"My body is nearly gone, and it is difficult for me to think. I do not have much time — none of us do. The world has reached a critical threshold." Wilam stopped the computer circuits from transmitting his physical pain, but Marek knew intuitively how much he was suffering. "For a long time it has been teetering between revivification and ultimate destruction. It was put in that position purposely by the Ancients. These — these are concepts that are beyond your comprehension, Marek. You have not yet had the training. But Sheena — "

Wilam struggled to keep his synapses open.

"You should rest — "

"No! There is no time. There are things Sheena needs to know but not until she finds the Sacred Portal. That is of utmost import — " He faltered again; his mind was fading. "Marek, I solved some of the riddles. I was close to discovering the truth about our world. Very close. But I was missing some essential codes.

Entropy

Now, her data have corroborated my theories and have given me those codes. The explanation is so simple — "

"Wilam please — "

"Let me think! Let me — think." Thoughts flowed directly from Wilam's mind into Marek's — alien thoughts, imponderable thoughts, unconnected to anything that made sense to the young protégé; he had not yet the knowledge as a basis of understanding.

" — gravity is not only a force, but a measure of local space-time curvature: a distortion of the very nature of time and space.

" — this castle was once the command center and quarters for the leadership infrastructure.

" — the end of the world is not its demise, but a new beginning.

" — cylindrical.

" — without material objects neither space nor time can exist.

" — one way a wall, the other —

" — life is not just a consequence of nature; it is as much a part of nature as the stars and planets.

" — a spear have two ends? Does an arrow — ?

" — there will be life.

" — enter the vortex without fear. It is the only way to salvation.

" — down is out, up is in.

" — Marek!"

"I am here, Wilam. I am with you."

"Marek, I have imprinted all these data on the transfile that Sheena brought me. I have included all my notes, a lifetime of study, all that I am, my very essence. You must take it with you."

"Take it where?"

"To the Sacred Portal. You will need the codes to open the guarded gate."

"But — "

"You must go, before Charel takes control of the Council. He is mad for power. You know how many people he has already killed, how your father wallows in prison. If Charel gains control he will destroy us all.

That is why I fear him more than anything. He knows more than he allows — "

Marek was frightened. Wilam rambled about the Sacred Portal as if it were a real place. "But how can I do this?"

"Find Sheena, and help her. She knows the way. The Sacred Portal is at the other end of the world. That is where you must go."

"But — "

"And when — you get — there, my boy — I will be — with you."

The transfile emerged from its slot.

"Wilam! Wilam!"

The great scientist's program terminated; his body no longer moved. Marek initiated an emergency override coding sequence, so he could enter Wilam's personal file and reopen communication links. But no matter how hard he searched, he found nothing but a vast electronic emptiness. The tenuous cohesion of organic energy, the synaptic flow that had once been the soul of a living person, had collapsed, and there was no way to resurrect it. All that remained was a memory.

Marek suffered a grief more profound than when, as a lad, his mother had been killed by a Council member's motor cart.

He was distraught. Worse, he was alone — more alone than he had ever been in his life. And the loneliness scared him. Without Wilam, without his father, he had no one to turn to. He disconnected the input leads and sank to the floor, giving in to his sorrow; he was incapable, in fact, of fighting it off.

He had less time to himself than he needed. The commotion at the door was barely enough warning for action. Quickly he crawled into the repair module beneath the console, cowering as Charel entered the chamber with his ever-present contingent.

"At last, he is dead, thanks to my impetuous son. Although I would have preferred to have him divine a few more secrets before passing on. But, what is done, is done. You, send the alarm that Marek is on the loose and must be captured at once. You, gather up these instruments and take them to my room. Hurry, there is no time to lose."

Then they were gone.

Marek emerged from hiding in shame, shaking uncontrollably. He was acting like a boy instead of the man he wanted to become. Had not Wilam taught him that courage was a virtue only one step removed from righteousness? With his master's will in mind, Marek pulled himself together. He yanked out the transfile and stuffed it in his pouch.

Wilam had never let him down: he had schooled him well, shared his thoughts, confided his feelings, and protected him from the evil of the Council. Marek could do no less for him.

Whether or not there actually *was* a Sacred Portal was not for him to decide. Marek would undertake its quest because it was his mentor's final plea.

He feared demons and savages and palace guards, he feared the unknown beyond the castle walls, he feared the length of the terrible journey and the treacherous obstacles blocking the way. But most of all, he feared that he would not measure up to Sheena's standards.

She was his idol.

Chapter 21

"Help! Help!" Samel pleaded. "I be floating."

Marek scurried off the road into the weeds, grabbed the boater, and pulled him down. "Are you hurt?"

"Only me pride." Samel tossed aside the wad of twigs that had torn loose from the plant he had been holding onto. "I be needing something a bit more substantial to hold me down — if down have meaning any more."

As an oddity of observational perspective, the moving land that no longer seemed to slide, neither any longer seemed to rise. Although the tread-accepting road was a horizontal extension of the ascending road from the sea, the slope was lost to perception as if it had leveled out without notice. The trees yielded to a dense field of tangled shrubbery with no relief or change in elevation until now.

Sheena crept along the road using the tread depressions for grips. "Once we enter the tunnel you need not worry about floating off."

The top of the cliff was lost in fog, as were the rock walls extending to either side. Multifaceted crystals embedded in stone sparkled brilliantly despite the lack of polish. The road entered the cliff at its base. The tunnel, large enough to accommodate an armored carriage, was a jewel-lined kaleidoscope of seemingly infinite length.

"There be dents in the walls and ceiling." Freder launched himself through the air and into the tunnel. He rose effortlessly to the ceiling, gripped the indentations, and clung there as easily as if he had been lounging on the ground. "I be liking this new mode of travel."

Sheena found it unsettling to drift inside the glittering tube that knew not the constraints of gravity, and felt a twinge of nausea as she propelled herself along: it was disorienting to pass under Freder, who hung upside down while waiting for his companions to catch up. She pushed off lightly from one indentation to another, always maintaining contact with one of the tunnel's four surfaces. Marek followed suit.

The boaters seemed to enjoy the three-dimensional quality of freefall. Samel quickly lost his fear of floating off forever into the sky; he bounced from one side to the other like an acrobat in training.

"Flying be more fun than swimming. I be liking it." Samel alighted on the wall adjacent to Freder, and added, "As long as there be four walls around me."

Up and down no longer had any meaning in the objective sense: they were directions of choice dependent upon a person's momentary orientation. Up for one could be down for another; sides were interchangeable. Sheena found herself proceeding in a motion that was neither a skip nor a soar, but a combination of the two. And although the phenomenon of absolute weightlessness was unexplainable scientifically, taken in context with Erbridge's other marvels, it was just another piece of an inexplicable puzzle. Sheena simply accepted it.

Taking advantage of this new form of locomotion, the foursome moved along so fast that soon the entrance was a pinpoint behind them. Now they were in a tube with neither beginning nor end, start nor finish, like bacteria in a long straw. They traveled so long and so far that Sheena began to doubt that the tunnel had an outlet.

"There is a door blocking our path," Marek, ever alert, announced.

"It be moving," Freder added.

Samel was in mid-flight, coasting up the center of the tunnel. He immediately reached out, grabbed onto a dent, and slammed himself flat against a wall. "It be coming our way."

"It is not a door, but a carriage." Sheena gripped the floor depressions tighter, until she realized that the tracked vehicle would drive over her and crush her. "Quick! Get out of its way."

She leaped straight away from the road, hit the ceiling, and flattened her body against the crystalline surface. Marek landed next to her, stretched out like sailcloth. Freder took the wall opposite Samel.

A moment later, the carriage drove by with guns bristling but inactive. Its squared forepeak brushed Sheena's battle dress. The passenger tubs extended deep into the vehicle; the cargo compartment was empty. The carriage continued on its track without slowing or halting, motivated by some incomprehensible program written by the Ancients in an age long past.

Sheena stretched out full length. "The end of the tunnel is near."

"And perhaps the end of our journey?" Marek added hopefully.

"We will soon know."

Freder and Samel repressed their natural boater's inclination to clown around. Even far from home and the sea, they exhibited definite lack of expectation: theirs was not a world of certain doubt, but of naive acceptance. To them a voyage never terminated in success or failure; to them a voyage was simply motion: the representation of life. The end of one voyage blended into the beginning of another. Sheena tried hard to accept that philosophy because everything she had learned about the world led her to believe that Erbridge was on a similar voyage.

The tunnel suddenly opened up into an immense room that was the epitome of technology. Huge transformers suspended from cables, and spouting impossibly long insulator poles, could not have existed under normal weight conditions. Motors mounted sideways and upside down were stark reminders of the peculiar state of weightlessness. Oddly missing were the catenary curves of high voltage conductors.

Work stations, parts cabinets, benches, tool chests, drafting tables, and all the instruments and paraphernalia that were part of a proper maintenance station hung at various levels interconnected by grooved platforms that stretched vertically and horizontally in a complicated three-dimensional web. There was order

Entropy

here, and constant movement. Sliding along wires were mechanical boxes with articulated appendages that collected tools, made adjustments, and replaced worn parts.

"By the Ancients, the whole place be automated." Freder scampered along a notched girder to a landing high above the floor. The effort exerted was minimal. "It be a factory in the sky and the foundry of the Ancients."

Electrical collectors an order of magnitude larger than any in the castle subbasements spread out so far before them that they resembled island mounts puncturing a boundless burnished ocean.

Samel tried to take it all in. "There be enough power here to move the world."

Sheena gripped more tightly the tread indentations; she was afraid of falling up, of losing contact with the floor and floating out of control. "Let us follow the track."

"Which one?" Marek indicated tunnel exits on either side of the one from which they had emerged. Each had a track that penetrated the maze of machinery and generating equipment. "Or do they all lead to the same place?"

Sheena shrugged.

"At least it be easy travel for a person used to the rigors of the sea." Samel charged forward from grip to grip, having learned his lesson about losing touch. "But I be cautious."

Sheena could feel the electrical potential in the air as she scudded beneath (above?) the transformer nodes. She reasoned that anywhere the carriage could go, so could she. There was not likely to be overt danger in the hall of the Ancients, especially when the doors were left open. In her mind, the argument that people were nothing more than laboratory animals was in doubt. One does not let the experiment contaminate the experimenter.

She led the way through a maze of ladders and scaffolds and hovering machinery. Beyond were electrical distribution panels by the thousands. Gold bus bars as thick as quivers rose like a gilded forest, conducting tremendous voltages from sources under the floor to somewhere above the confusing network of wire highways.

"It is all operational." Marek surveyed the three-dimensional electrical distribution system with awe. There was no ceiling and no obscuring fog. Instead the incredible array of machinery and wire mesh locomotion guides aspired to heights with such increasing complexity that eventually individual units shrank to toys attached to slender filaments.

"It is more magnificent than I could possibly have imagined." Sheena was humbled to her very core. How long they crawled along the straight track through the colossal grandeur she could not determine. She was lost in awe at the scope and constant spectacle of ancient construction.

Eventually, they reached a barricade.

It was a simple, smooth unadorned wall whose breadth and height were lost amid the free-hanging mechanical structures and wire stabilizers that filled the intra-tunnel world. Sheena still could not determine whether they were inside a vast cavern, or simply on the opposite side of a rock wall that the tunnel had led them through.

"The track be leading to a gate," Samel noted.

"Aye, like the bulkheads separating the underground highway chambers."

Marek pulled himself up (away from the floor) a grooved girder, and from that along a platform to a control cubicle. After a moment's inspection: "I can jumper the security circuit and unlock the gate. But hang on in case the other side is a vacuum."

Sheena and the boatmen wrapped themselves around perpendicular support wires that were stretched as taut as steel beams. Sheena waved to Marek. "Do it."

Marek touched the jumper wire across two terminals. The hatch unsealed itself and slid aside on well-oiled rollers. There was no pressure differential. Sheena released her hold on the wire, pushed herself off, and coasted through the opening into a huge parking garage that contained none of the convoluted wiring and piping; the chamber was completely devoid of everything except motorized carriages parked in charging bays.

To the side, Sheena noticed that a carriage track was laid under a hatch identical to the open one behind. Adjacent to that lay another track, and beyond that another equidistantly placed — all the way around the upward curving floor. Tracks were even emplaced along the ceiling, and continued right on around the room and back down the other side. Without any obscuring mechanical works, it was readily apparent how the carriage tracks converged in front almost to a point. For one dizzying moment, Sheena had the feeling that she was crouched upon the rim of a gigantic funnel, that the tracks entered the top of the funnel and ran down to a circular stopper at the base; or, she just as easily imagined that the funnel was upside down converging on a point above. Or was it sideways? It was an illusion, she hoped, inspired by the duration of weightlessness.

"This be the weirdest place," Freder commented.

"No." Marek floated into the garage and studied his surroundings. "It is exactly as Wilam predicted. All roads lead to the Sacred Portal. We have nearly reached the end of the world, beyond which we can go no farther."

"A sphere has no end," Sheena argued.

"Wilam's later interpretation of the shape of the world was not necessarily yours. He had strange ideas about curvature, something he called concavity. In his final ramblings, he formulated the notion that you had in fact visited the wall at the end of the world, the implication being that the world must have another end. I believe we have arrived."

"Nonsense." Sheena stopped in her tracks, or rather, those designed for the treads of the wayward carriage. The many dialogues and discussions she and

Marek had held during their long sojourn rushed through her mind. Sheena had never once wavered from her avowed purpose to cross the world and find the Sacred Portal. There was no uncertainty on that account. Yet deep within, she knew that her concept of what the Sacred Portal might be was abstract in the extreme.

Marek passed her by. "I pity you, Sheena, for you do not have the advantage of ignorance. I can only repeat one of your father's favorite aphorisms: the vane intellectual knows it all, the merely wise keeps an open mind."

"Well put, but what does it mean?" Sheena rushed to keep up with him.

"You once told me that I needed more than trust, that I needed faith. I now repeat that to you." Marek reached the empty revetment belonging to the carriage that had almost squashed them in the tunnel. Next to it was a hatch with an override switch. "What we find on the other side of this door may not be what you have anticipated. But it is what we came here to find."

Sheena drew herself to her full height, maintaining only a slender hold on the grooved floor. "I have the courage of my convictions, you have the strength of your ignorance." She hovered lightly, reverently, understanding with dread the naked truth behind Marek's statement. A lifetime of expectation was about to be revealed. She steeled herself for either disappointment or revelation. "Open it."

Freder and Samel huddled close as Marek pressed the switch. The door opened immediately. No one moved.

The chamber was twice the size of the courtyard at castle Erbridge, and crammed with more electronic gadgetry than all the castles combined. Thousands of computer consoles extended around the room and up to the faraway ceiling like some vast three-dimensional control center. Bank after bank of annunciator panels vibrant with life broadcasted constantly changing data. It was a communications link and mainframe assembly

Entropy

of mammoth proportions. All that was missing were operators. The entire complex was automated and still operating.

"By the Ancients," Freder proclaimed, with admiration and astonishment.

"Undoubtedly." Sheena sailed into the room by shuffling along a notched aisle, trying hard not to be intimidated by the incredible array of technology. She felt as if she had been atomized and was groping through the miniaturized workings of an alien computer, like a single bit of information following a programmed path through some incomprehensible electronic circuit.

"Be this the Sacred Portal?" Samel wanted to know.

"No, we have yet to open the guarded gate." Marek reached into his pouch and drew out the transfile Wilam had entrusted to him. "This is our key." He floated effortlessly into the control center. "If only we can find the lock."

Sheena led the way through the labyrinthine framework, past concentric rings of consoles and display boards that blinked onerously, along the aisle converging gradually with others on either side, toward the golden, glittering gangway that drew her hypnotically, as if she were a mindless metal filing attracted to a divine magnet. Each thrust brought her closer to the nozzle at the bottom (top?) of the funnel; the circle of computer stations shrank in diameter.

At last she poised weightlessly at the small end of the funnel. The aisles on either side likewise terminated at the edge of a sharply upturned ramp that was like a ridge on the inside point of a cone. In front of her (or, from a different perspective, at the bottom of the cone) was a sunken annulus at which each aisle terminated. In the middle was a round hatch that seemed to Sheena like the focal point of the entire world.

And by the hatch, tethered to the central computer console by a set of input leads, hovered the remains of a warrior.

Freder and Samel spread out, each drifting to opposite sides of the hatch. Marek floated over the rim. Only Sheena approached the body devoid of flesh. For a long time she studied the loose folds of armor, the tattered battledress. Quivering, she bent to examine at close range the familial badge attached to the cloth. It was identical to her own.

She throbbed with emotion, and her body stung with the sharp pulse of electric shock. She lost control of herself and nearly went to pieces. Then she accepted the situation that she had prepared herself for all along. She sang a private prayer to the dead.

"Mother made it this far."

Slowly, Marek sidled up to Sheena and wrapped himself around her. He was sympathetic and loving. "May she rest forever in peace."

There was a long moment of reverence. Sheena's sorrow knew no bounds. But the time came to pass when she knew she must go on; she had great things to do. She pulled herself together, snatched the transfile away from Marek, and inserted it into the solitary slot. The response to the procedure was immediate.

"Hello, my baby."

Sheena reacted without knowing what she was doing. "Father!"

The commlink required no input cables. Communication was transmitted through the very air.

"Sorry to shake you up this way, Sheena, but there was no way to warn you. Nor did I have time to brief Marek on what the transfile contained."

"What — what does it contain? And how can you — be here?"

"I am not here, my baby. I am merely a construct — a program that I wrote over my own personality file. Oh, no doubt I appear real to you. But do not be deceived. The transfile is nothing more than magnetic configurations, a memory pattern, a data file, written in such a way that access can be obtained by question and answer instead of by fusion and program search. I have written you in here as well, so our programs can interact in lifelike fashion. Have I accomplished that inter-

Entropy

action?"

Sheena swore she could feel her father's presence. It was an eerie sensation. "Only too well."

"Good. I thought it would make it easier for you. Even now I am encoding the matrix that will unlock the guarded gate. By locking in the transfile you have merged my program with Erbridge's master program. I have complete and instantaneous access to all the knowledge of the Ancients: the great race of people who built this place and put us here. Now I know for certain that we are their descendants, entrusted with a goal long forgotten. Your mother discovered this, too, but died trying to decipher the code of event initiation."

"Father, she is — her body lies here before us."

"Oh, my baby, I apologize for my ignorance. I have no external sensory inputs."

Now Sheena knew for certain that her father was not real. His sentiments were sincere but the inflection of true feeling was absent. The program contained only his intellectual persona: the dispassion of pure thought. He had been transformed by death into an automaton with only the semblance of animation. In a way she was relieved, for death once accepted was difficult to repudiate. Sheena was mature enough to accept the truth that life means change, that the past cannot be revived, that each moment is a new beginning, that the world of the adult is never equal to the dream of the child.

She shrugged off the mournful impact of finding her mother's long dead body, of communicating with the thoughts of her deceased father. She treated those emotions like subdued nostalgia brought on by perusing the family album. She had to, or she would go mad. If she felt sadness, it was because her mother had fallen short of her ambitions, or because her father was not truly alive to share the joy of ultimate success. She could serve their memory best by achieving what they had both set out to accomplish.

"I understand." She could not now bring herself to refer to him as Father. She was, after all, conversing with a program written by Wilam, not with the person himself. The fact that the program displayed his mannerisms served on an emotional level to make it more difficult for her to operate. In that assessment, Wilam had been wrong. "What must we do to open the Sacred Portal? What is the meaning of the Great Expanse?"

"Questions that were once philosophical have at last become practical. The whole rationale for our being revolves around a space-time singularity, practically all that survives of the immeasurable sea of vacuum once populated by planets and stars and galaxies . . . "

Sheena's mind was filled with fleeting images which, despite their brevity, produced indisputable understanding: of the gigantic explosion that augured the beginning of the Universe, of the coalescence of matter, of the formation of stars and planets, of the evolution of life, of the gravitational pull that finally ended expansion, of reversal and ultimate collapse. The panorama flowed from beginning to end with an infinite number of stages in between. And she retained it all.

"That be quite a tale." Freder wavered like a tall blade of grass caught by the wind. "But it be making sense." After a pause, "Somehow."

Came another splurge of images: of a rotating cylinder spiraling into a mass so dense that no electromagnetic radiation escaped its surface, of protruding power collectors that siphoned raw energy from the event horizon of a naked singularity, of instability caused by increasing proximity, of the ultimate destruction that would result if the escape procedure were not activated.

Samel temporarily lost his anchorage and drifted away. "Stop! Stop! It be too much for me poor brain."

But the images would not stop. Sheena lived every moment of the Ancients' story: how they designed the double hull with its self-sealing coagulant, how they constructed the transparent zone beneath the ocean, how they bisected the living area with a mountainous bulkhead and how the venturi effect kept its emergency sealing surface clean, how they planted the forests and jungles and swamps on the cylinder's inner lining, how they populated the castles, and why there was a wall at the other end of the world . . . "

Marek fathomed the world's secret. "Erbridge is a starboat."

And it was plunging into a vortex where mass and energy had no meaning, where space and time were warped into a different reality. The ultimate marvel of the Ancients' technology was the utilization of the singularity's massive spun-off energy supply to generate a field of force to protect the cylinder from the destructive strength of gravity and the tidal effect. But as Erbridge approached the event horizon, the force-field generators were strained beyond their capacity to repulse magnetic induction and negate the effects of gravity; radiation leaked through the outer shields.

"So we are nothing more than an experiment?" was Sheena's immediate interpretation. "Our ancestors were sent on a one-way trip to study this singularity. Now we-their-descendants are expected to transmit the data to the Ancients waiting safely beyond the grip of dissolution. And we are to die in the process."

"You do not fully understand," came Wilam's programmed thoughts. "We have a purpose much more profound . . . "

"Sheena!"

Marek's warning shook her out of her contemplative mode, and impeded the transference of further data. Where he pointed was a danger more immediately pertinent than the destruction of the world.

With calm resignation Sheena drew her sword. "Charel."

As the evil Council member disembarked from the carriage, the rest of his contingent drifted close from the rear. Charel crouched behind his personal bodyguards, his injuries preventing him from holding a sword. But the others approached with pikes and upthrust blades.

"At last we meet again, Sheena. Only this time there is nowhere for you to go." The guards spread out and encircled the foursome. "You cannot escape me."

Sheena refused to be intimidated. "How did you track us?"

"I did not. I had my own map. And since all roads lead to the Sacred Portal, it was inevitable that we should come together at journey's end."

"What do you know about the Sacred Portal? Why do you seek it?"

"For one who is about to die you ask many questions."

"We are all about to die, Charel. Some sooner than others." She wielded her sword threateningly even though the Council member was protected and not within reach. "The fortunate will be reborn."

"Do you really believe that? Do you believe the Sacred Portal is the way to salvation? Or is your madness preyed upon by your father's delusions?"

Sheena was too close to the finish line to let herself be perturbed by Charel's accusations. The great seal guarding the gate to the Sacred Portal was slowly unlatching. She remained calm and unemotional. "You tried these tactics before, Charel."

"I underestimated you, Sheena, as did my son. But I never underestimated your father. He was a genius and, like all true geniuses, misguided. That was why I eavesdropped on his programs. Only by knowing one's enemy can one hope to overcome him. Wilam provided raw data whose veracity I do not question. It was our conclusions that differed. He wanted to believe that the Sacred Portal is a gateway to everlasting life, so he believed it. But the truth is that it is a transference device that confers a sentence of immediate death."

Sheena was suddenly uneasy. Were the Ancients indifferent to the fate of their progeny? Were they willing to sacrifice innocent lives in their search for knowledge? Did her father know Erbridge's true significance, or was he deluded by his own precepts of goodness? Or was this just another of Charel's cunning feints?

"Then what is it you want?"

"I want you to understand that your real adversaries are those who put us here, that once we give them the information they desire, we are doomed — our usefulness ended. Our survival depends upon our insularity. If you activate the hidden mechanisms the signal will be transmitted and Erbridge will be destroyed. Lock the guarded gate, Sheena, and throw away the key. To do otherwise will kill us all.

Sheena swayed. Charel's elocution contained the possibility of truth. But what was Wilam's program about to reveal?

The coding sequence was completed. The hatch to which Katha's remains were attached slid out like a telescoping tube. Crystals embedded on the cylindrical surface sparkled hypnotically, surrounding the initiation device that needed only to be pressed.

Wilam's program contradicted Charel's arguments. "The Ancients were a wise people, a moral people; not ones to bestow death upon their descendants. They sacrificed their lives for us. The Universe of which we are a part is nearing extinction. It is contracting into the seed from which it was born, and when it does, there will be no space, no time, no reality — only a state of eternal nothingness. And of the billions of billions of life forms in the Universe, only the inhabitants of Erbridge will escape this oncoming and inevitable nonexistence. You must — "

Charel interrupted. "He is wrong — dead wrong. Do not be deceived by his rationalizations. The time of quakes will pass even as they have come, and stability in time will return to the world."

"Not true, Charel. If Erbridge is allowed to continue on its course, it will be torn apart by the tremendous force of gravity that for generations has been overpowering the machines that convert the event horizon's energy to a protective force field. Eventually, the world will be torn apart by tidal forces, and what is left of Erbridge will fall into the singularity and cease to exist. All the planning of the Ancients will have been for naught."

"Deactivate the guarded gate before it is too late,

Sheena. Join me. With this power under our control, we can govern not just castle Erbridge, but world Erbridge. That is our future. That is our destiny."

Sheena did not make the mistake of being distracted by Charel's oratory prattle. She noticed the guards closing in. She also knew what she had to do; she was beyond being dissuaded by debate. She had begun her trek with confidence in its justification, and, although she was confused by experiences encountered along the way, she had to complete the journey begun so long ago.

Hers was not an act of reason, but of faith.

She drifted back toward the activator. At the first sign of intent, Charel signaled his troops. The mass movement triggered an immediate response from the crossbow wielders; three arrows thwacked through the air. Because the guards were spread out, they made easy targets, and three of them were pierced with agonizing accuracy; armor was no defense against high-speed, steel-tipped arrows. The rest of the guards drew themselves together in typical defensive posture, and charged.

"Stop her!"

Sheena dodged the ill-thrown pikes that flew weightlessly through the air. Marek and Freder and Samel reloaded and shot again, each taking out his adversary. Then the guards were upon them. Freder lashed out with his sword and stabbed one guard through the left torso; the wounded guard deflated quickly into a shapeless mass. Freder and Samel proved unerringly adept at ducking swords and undercutting with their daggers between the scales of offending armor. Some of their scales were severed at the roots. Once thrust aside, the dead guards floated out of the fighting arena.

Due to the sheer number of attackers, two guards got through the three-person perimeter and drifted straight toward Sheena, their swords slicing wildly. She pulled herself together, swung her blade defiantly, and hacked off one guard's sword-wielding tentacle. The other she stabbed between torsos, cutting them both; in agony he let himself go, and drifted off a bloody, amorphous mass.

Marek drew his sword and slashed two opponents one after the other. But two others closed upon him bodily and, if there had been any gravity, would have borne him down under their weight. Instead, all three of them bounced off the floor and rebounded into space. Marek strangled one with the great strength of his tentacles. The other he kicked with his expanding torsos and spun him out of the fight.

Freder was bloodied by a pike thrust that carved armor off his torso. Samel sank his knife into the piker's back and saved his companion from further injury. During the resulting melee, all went cartwheeling through the air.

While friend and foe were scattered around the chamber, Charel dashed after Sheena; she had already pounced upon the activator. He swung his tentacles from groove to groove until he crashed into her back and grappled for her sword. He had barely succeeded in twisting it against her when he was hit from behind by an enraged Marek, splayed out to his fullest extent. Charel struggled, but he was no match against Marek's great physique.

"You once ordered me to kill, Charel, and I promised to carry out your orders." Marek wrapped his tentacles around the Council member's torsos. He spread himself out and pulled in opposite directions. "It is with the greatest glee that I do so now."

Charel squirmed as his torsos were stretched apart. "You will — kill us — all — you fools."

"No, you would let us die out of your greed for power." Marek exerted his strength effortlessly. "Despite the vastness of the Great Expanse, there is no room for your kind."

"Sheena, stop him — "

Marek pulled beyond Charel's capacity to stay together. The Council member was torn in two and flung away like two empty sacks. "I pray that both our souls find mercy in the next universe."

Sheena's tentacles grappled with the activating mechanism. She exerted pressure and squeezed her body against the pad. For the computer program that had been waiting patiently for hundreds of generations, it took but the pulse of a single electron to initiate the decoupling procedure. Her mind was flooded with images.

Beyond the wall at the end of the world, a mass many times that of habitable Erbridge dropped below the event horizon — like the after section of the cutaway boat drawn to the bottom of the oceanic vortex that enabled the forward section to climb out of the well. The great rotating cylinder that still revolved around the singularity spun off at an interdimensional tangent through contorted space-time geometry and emerged into another universe — an expanding universe — that had a long time to go before it slowed, stopped, and reversed direction toward ultimate collapse. A universe where people had the opportunity to grow, and reproduce, and expand, and realize their full potential.

Without their leader, the guards ceased fighting. Freder and Samel danced in circles, expressing the joy of life and good fortune.

Marek threw his tentacles around Sheena, and hugged her with a passion that exhibited much more than relief.

For the first time in her life, Sheena, with the weight of responsibility lifted from her back, allowed the stirrings deep inside her to surface with conscious desire. She knew for certain that her mothering instincts were emerging. And she was certain that Marek would not mind making her a mother.

"We have come a long way, Marek, but we have a longer way to go. There is a world to rebuild, a people to reunite, a new generation to spawn. I propose that we do it together."

Marek was ecstatic. "I will be honored to carry your eggs."

Entropy

And somewhere in the back of her mind was a computer program named Wilam. Like all memories, it was one that would be there always. The individual can die, the body can waste away, but one's accomplishments live on forever.

That was the true meaning of immortality.

www.ingramcontent.com/pod-product-compliance
Ingram Content Group UK Ltd.
Pitfield, Milton Keynes, MK11 3LW, UK
UKHW041410180426
11947UKWH00007B/54